Dear Reader,

We're constantly striving to bring you the best romance fiction by the most exciting authors, and in Harlequin Romance® we're especially keen to feature fresh, sparkling, emotionally exhilarating novels! Modern love stories to suit your every mood: poignant, deeply moving stories; lively, upbeat romances with sparks flying; or sophisticated, edgy novels with a cosmopolitan flavor.

All our authors are special, and we hope you continue to enjoy each month's new selection of Harlequin Romance novels. This month we're delighted to feature another novel with extra fizz! Bestselling author Rebecca Winters brings us a fast-paced, feel-good romance that tells both sides of the story! The heroine, Rainey, and the hero, Payne, both get their say. And the result? A gripping, emotionally insightful read!

We hope you enjoy this book by Rebecca Winters—it's fresh, flirty and feel-good! And look out for future sparkling stories in Harlequin Romance. If you'd like to share your thoughts and comments with us, do please write to:

The Harlequin Romance Editors
Harlequin Mills & Boon Ltd.
Eton House, 18-24 Paradise Road
Richmond
Surrey TW9 1SR, U.K.
Or e-mail us at: tango@hmb.co.uk.

Happy reading!

The Editors

Rebecca Winters, an American writer and mother of four, is excited to be in this new millennium because it means another new beginning. Having said goodbye to the classroom, where she taught French and Spanish, she is now free to spend more time with the family, to travel and to write the Harlequin Romance® novels she loves so dearly.

Rebecca loves to hear from readers. If you wish to e-mail her, please visit her Web site at www.rebeccawinters-author.com.

Rebecca Winters has written over forty-five books for Harlequin Romance® and is an international bestselling author. Her wonderfully unique, sparkling stories continue to be immensely popular with readers around the world.

Books by Rebecca Winters

HARLEQUIN ROMANCE®
3703—THE PRINCE'S CHOICE
3710—THE BABY DILEMMA
3729—THE TYCOON'S PROPOSITION
3739—BRIDE FIT FOR A PRINCE
3743—RUSH TO THE ALTAR

MANHATTAN MERGER

Rebecca Winters

TANGO
IT TAKES TWO...

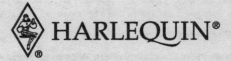

HARLEQUIN®

TORONTO • NEW YORK • LONDON
AMSTERDAM • PARIS • SYDNEY • HAMBURG
STOCKHOLM • ATHENS • TOKYO • MILAN • MADRID
PRAGUE • WARSAW • BUDAPEST • AUCKLAND

ISBN 0-373-03755-4

MANHATTAN MERGER

First North American Publication 2003.

Visit us at www.eHarlequin.com

Printed in U.S.A.

CHAPTER ONE

"Uncle Payne?"

Thirty-three-year-old Payne Sterling glanced up from the screen of his laptop in time to see his favorite niece Catherine come flying in the study. He doubted her feet touched the ground.

His fiancée followed at a little slower pace in her wheelchair. Both women seemed panicked by something.

"You've got to see this!"

Catherine looked and sounded frantic as she thrust a paperback book at him.

"Easy, sweetheart."

Puzzled, he took it from her, then gave it his full attention. To his surprise he discovered it was a romance novel of all things entitled *Manhattan Merger,* by Bonnie Wrigley.

Below the title was a picture of a man holding a woman in his arms. They were standing in the office of a New York City skyscraper where the Manhattan skyline was revealed in the background.

Upon a second look he realized it wasn't just any office.

Or any man...

Even though it wasn't a photograph, it was like looking at himself in a mirror.

He stared at it for a full minute in stunned disbelief.

"Promise you won't tell mother I've been reading these, Uncle Payne. The thing is, over the last year I've noticed that quite a few of the men on the covers resemble you. But this one *is* you," Catherine's voice trembled. "Even his hairline is the same shape."

He could see that.

"She's right, Payne!" Diane cried out anxiously. "This man has your build and dark brown hair. It's the same length. Everything is like you, even to the exact hue of your blue eyes. That's why I told Catherine she had to show this romance to you."

Both of them had lost color.

"He's even dressed in the same kind of suit and shirt I've noticed you wear to work before, Uncle Payne! And that view out of those same kinds of windows is exactly what you see when you walk in your office. The person who did the cover has to know a lot of private things about you.

"Look!" She pointed to some items. "See that picture of a ship passing in front of a lighthouse? You have a similar picture hanging on your office wall! And what about that little picture of a bulldog propped on the desk?"

Payne had recognized those details at once, but he hadn't wanted to say anything for fear of alarming either of them further.

The fact that he'd hired an architect to incorporate the old lighthouse at Crag's Head into a home where he'd been living for the past few years had set off more warning bells.

He eyed his fifteen-year-old niece whose hair was the same pale gold as his sister's. "Have you read this yet?"

"No— As soon as I showed it to Diane, we decided to bring it straight to you!"

"You did the right thing."

Somewhere he'd heard it said everyone had a look-alike. Possibly more than one. Maybe this was a fantastic coincidence, but he couldn't take any chances. Not after what had happened at Christmas.

"Where do you get these books, Catherine?"

"One of the maids reads them first, then gives me a bunch. When I'm through, I return them to her."

"Which maid?"

"Nyla."

"Catherine really shouldn't be reading books like this, Payne," Diane declared. "Whoever is responsible for putting you on the covers probably read a lot of trashy romances at a young age and can no longer distinguish between fantasy and reality."

"There's nothing trashy about them," Catherine defended quietly. "They're exciting stories about people falling in love. You learn so much and go so many places. I think they're wonderful! If you or mom would ever take the time to read one, you'd be hooked too."

Diane's eyes sent him a private message that indicated her strong disapproval.

"Listen, Uncle Payne—don't be angry with Nyla. I don't want her to get into trouble. She's the one who said I ought to bring it to your attention!

"If you say anything to mom and dad about this, they'll make me stay with grandma and grandpa the next time they take a trip. Nyla might even lose her job."

He shook his head. "I'm not going to jeopardize her position here. On the contrary, I want to thank Nyla for aiding and abetting you in your latest reading frenzy. It has brought something to light that needs to be dealt with right away."

Diane trembled. "This could be another crazed woman who's been following you around without your knowledge. There's no question she's been in your office, Payne. I'm afraid for you."

His fiancée had every reason to be terrified.

Less than six months ago Diane Wylie had taken a stalker's bullet meant for him and was now condemned to a wheelchair—perhaps permanently.

Consumed by guilt, Payne moved around the desk and hunkered down at her side. Reaching for her hand he said, "I don't know what to believe at the moment, but if this is another demented wacko, I'm going to find out. You two stay here. I'll be back soon."

He stood up, stroked his niece's pale cheek, then grabbed the romance off the desk and strode out of his brother-in-law's study. A few minutes later he caught up with Nyla in the kitchen enjoying afternoon tea with some of the other staff.

Her expression sobered when he showed her the romance and asked where she'd bought it.

"I get them through a book club, but you can find copies people have already read at the used book store in the village. It's called Candle Glow Books. They have everything."

"Thank you, Nyla."

"You're welcome. I might as well tell you, I've seen your face on other covers, but your hair and eyes were always different. Until this book came in the mail, I thought it was just one of those amazing coincidences.

"I suggested Catherine say something to you about it. The likeness to you is startling! So's the story."

The story too?

Without wasting more time he pulled out his cell phone and called security to meet him around the back of his sister's house.

Since the age of seventeen, Payne had been the victim of half a dozen stalking incidents which had been brought to an end through police intervention.

But last December between Christmas and New Year, a psychotic woman had managed to penetrate the Sterling compound on Long Island's South Fork. Whether she came by water or managed to get past the guard at the gate, no one knew.

At the time, the Sterlings were having dinner for the Wylies who'd invited them to their home for brunch earlier in the day. The Wylies lived on the North Shore of Long Island and had enjoyed this exchange tradition with the Sterlings for many years.

Prior to the Christmas holidays Payne had been out of the country a great deal and had spent most it working at his office where he could catch up on the paperwork in solitude.

While immersed, his mother called him upset because he'd missed the Wylies' brunch. Could she at least count on him for dinner, and would he please bring Diane who was in the city shopping? If she could fly back with him, then no one would be late.

Knowing how much his mother cared about these things, he agreed to come and bring Diane with him. As the two of them were walking from the car to the front porch of his parents' home, the demented intruder had emerged from the bushes. The thirtyish-looking woman claimed to be in love with Payne. If she couldn't have him, no other woman could either.

Payne saw the glint of metal in time to push Diane aside before the gun went off, but the stalker had poor aim. To his horror the bullet struck Diane in her lower back before he could knock the lunatic to the ground. The horrific experience had changed all their lives.

Diane had clung to him all the way to the hospital. In the fear that she was going to die, she'd told him how much she needed him, how much she'd always loved him.

He'd had no idea of her deep feelings for him. He'd never been interested in her that way, but at that point it didn't matter because he couldn't have abandoned her in the state she was in.

Several months later she still couldn't walk though she retained some feeling in her legs. The doctors told her they'd done all they could do and suggested she go to a clinic in Switzerland reputed to have success with her kind of spinal injury.

Afraid of failure, Diane had flatly refused to consider it and wouldn't be consoled. At that point Payne took stock of his life and decided that if he proposed marriage, she might be more inclined to get the help she needed.

But after their engagement was announced, she seemed to retreat further into herself, unwilling to discuss going to Switzerland. Worse, she'd developed an almost irrational fear of the two of them being shot again.

In order to reassure her, Payne had made certain new security measures had been added to protect her and the Wylies as well as everyone on the Sterling estate. His fiancée now had twenty-four-hour protection.

As for Payne, four security men accompanied him wherever he went on business. A helicopter took him to his office in Manhattan. If he had to fly overseas, he used his private jet. When he had to drive somewhere on Long Island, one of the security men chauffeured him in a bulletproof limousine with one-way glass windows.

En route to the used bookstore in Oyster Bay, he handed the novel to the retired Navy SEAL, Mac, who'd been his personal bodyguard for the last three years.

"What do you make of this?"

Mac took one look and whistled. His gray eyes darted to Payne in puzzlement before he gave it back to him. "How come *you're* on the cover?"

"That's what I intend to find out."

While the driver looked for Candle Glow Books, Payne opened the novel to the copyright page.

Red Rose Romance Publishers, Inc., Second Avenue, New York, New York.

His eyes narrowed. He'd never heard of it, but that location was east of Central Park near the Turtle Bay Grill where he often met with overseas clients.

It appeared the book had been published two months ago.

That meant whatever party was responsible for his picture being on the cover had possessed knowledge of him long before the publication date. Most publishing houses had up to three or more years of books waiting to go to press.

There was a disclaimer.

Any characters, names or incidents in this book do not exist outside the mind of the author.

Like hell!

A grimace marred Payne's features.

He turned the book over to read the blurb. By the time he'd digested the second sentence, his body had broken out in a cold sweat.

Secrets?

Powerful, dashing New York billionaire Logan Townsend, is hiding a painful secret from his fiancée and family.

"Good Lord," he whispered.

When he's involved in an accident in the Canyonlands of the American West, Dr. Maggie Osborn discovers what that secret is.

Unbeknownst to him, she puts her life in danger to save his.

But secrets have a way of getting out.

It isn't until Logan returns to New York that he learns Maggie is keeping one from him.

On the verge of sealing the most vital merger of his existence, he's torn between duty and desire.

Upon reading the last line, Payne felt as if someone had just walked over his grave. Convinced nothing about this book was an accident, he rolled it up in his fist.

He would willingly litter the island page by page to be rid of it. But for several obvious reasons he couldn't do that and was forced to sit there while he attempted to contain the savage impulse.

Sam, the security man at the wheel, turned down an alley, then came to a stop at the rear of the used book store in question. Two of the security men, John and Andy, jumped out to enter the shop ahead of Payne.

It was near the closing hour on a Tuesday evening in June. The timing couldn't have been more perfect if he'd hoped to avoid a lot of unwanted attention.

When the all clear was given, Mac covered Payne's back as they got out of the limousine and went inside the claustrophobic shop. It was a maze of cubbyholes and narrow aisles. With novels stacked to the ceiling everywhere he turned, there was no doubt this was a paperback lover's paradise.

The eyes of the older saleswoman behind the counter lit up at his approach. ''Mr. Sterling— Good evening! I'm Alice Perry. It's a real honor to have you in my store.'' She extended her hand which he shook.

''It's nice to meet you, Ms. Perry,'' he answered back.

''What can I do for you?''

He handed her the novel which would never lie flat again.

She took one look at it and her gaze lifted to his with excitement. ''I *knew* this was you!'' she cried. ''Every romance reader who's come in here lately has been talking about it.''

Payne groaned. ''According to my niece, there are other novels besides this that appear to have my likeness on the cover.''

''Oh there are!'' she blurted. ''But *this* one…''

So neither Catherine or Nyla had exaggerated anything. The news was going from bad to worse.

''At this point there isn't a copy of *Manhattan Merger* to be had anywhere on the Atlantic seaboard. My phone's been ringing off the hook with book dealers wanting copies! Those people lucky enough to have purchased it when it first came out are holding on to it for dear life.

"I kept copies of it and those other books for myself and my daughter who helps me run the shop. Perhaps before you leave you'd be willing to sign them? We'd be so thrilled if you would."

"I'd be happy to oblige, *if* I'd given my permission to appear on their covers."

Her smile faded. "I don't understand."

"Neither do I, Ms. Perry. That's why I'm here, to try and solve this mystery."

"You mean they just went ahead and used your picture?"

"I don't know, but I'm going to find out." He had to tamp down hard on his anger. "May I see them please?"

"I only have four left. They're locked away in the back room until a book dealer from Connecticut arrives on Friday. He's a collector and is going to pay me five thousand dollars apiece for them. Give me a moment and I'll bring them out."

"Only five thousand?" Mac said in a teasing whisper as the woman disappeared.

Ignoring the aside, Payne wandered over to the nearest bookshelf marked Mysteries. It was crammed with titles by various authors and sorted according to the alphabet. He pulled one out, curious to see what kind of cover was on the front.

The photograph had captured a busy street scene somewhere in London. A quick look at the copyright page gave the name of a British publisher.

He moved to another section marked Upbeat

Romances published in Los Angeles. Their covers were done in cartoon caricatures.

"Here we are."

He reshelved the book and joined the woman who'd laid the four books out on the counter for him. At first glance, he was horrified.

It was his face all right.

One of them depicted him as a Norseman with a flowing mane of white-blond hair, hazel eyes, bulging thighs and biceps twice his size. The book was called *Roald's Bride.*

Another showed him as a Castilian prince in royal ceremonial robes with pitch-black hair and eyes entitled, *Her Prince of Dreams.*

In the third book, *Undercover Love,* he was a gray-eyed Royal Canadian Mountie in full red dress uniform wearing a hat that covered his hair.

The Star Grazer was the last book. It portrayed him as a man from the future with auburn hair and brown eyes.

On all of the covers he had his arms around a beautiful woman. It appeared the same person had done the artwork.

"That's some life you lead," came another crack from Mac, sotto voce.

Payne made no response as he looked at the spines. All four were a product of Red Rose Romance Publishers, and had been printed within the last year.

"How many publishers put out paperback romances besides Red Rose?"

"Dozens of companies throughout the world, but the ones on my shelves come mainly from the United States,

England and Canada. Red Rose produces the most every year by quite a margin.''

"Have you seen my face on the covers of any romances other than Red Rose?"

"No."

That was the only good news so far. He could hope Red Rose was a mom-and-pop outfit that probably didn't have a large distribution base. "Do you have your romances sorted by publisher?"

"Yes."

"Will you show me where the romance section is?"

She laughed. "It's practically the whole shop except for the mysteries and science fiction here at the front."

He tried hard not to reveal his shock. "Why don't we try the Red Rose section first."

"Follow me, Mr. Sterling."

She led him a fourth of the way back. "It starts here and goes to the rear of the store."

His eyes widened in incredulity. "*These* are all Red Rose Romances?"

"Yes. Their company has nine different lines depending on what kind of romance you're looking for. Of course these are only the English versions. Their books are published in over a hundred languages. Something like that."

A hundred! That meant—

"We keep a few copies in Italian and Russian for the occasional visitor," she added.

He wondered how many times Catherine had been in here that her mother didn't know about. Payne loved his sister Phyllis, but like their mother, she didn't approve of a lot of things.

With her high-brow taste in the arts, music and literature, he doubted she'd ever had the curiosity to read a paperback romance. He couldn't help but wonder if Diane disliked them on principle too.

Or maybe she'd read a few when she was a teenager and refused to admit to it. He'd like to know.

In Payne's mind it would make Diane a more real person if she'd gone against her mother's wishes the way Catherine had done, and could own up to it...

"How far do some of these books date back?"

"Red Rose has been in business at least forty years that I know of."

Forty years?

He studied the voluminous amount of reading material. Evidently someone besides Nyla and Catherine had been gobbling these up by the thousands for at least four decades.

That was a long time... Too long not to be a reputable company.

"You'll find their books listed under the separate headings hanging from the ceiling over each section. There's something for every taste."

"So I see," Payne muttered.

A Touch of Romance, A Touch of Passion, A Touch of Espionage, A Touch of History, A Touch of Babies, A Touch of Royalty, A Touch of Sci-Fi/Paranormal, A Touch of Cowboy and *A Touch of Humor.*

"You're welcome to browse as long as you like."

"Thank you."

Since she'd pulled all the books with his likeness from the shelves, there was no point in sifting through the mountains of romances. The mere thought staggered the imagination.

However he did take a book from each section to examine the covers. All of them had been done as a painting rather than a photograph. He carried them to the counter.

"I'm going to buy these nine books. The four you're keeping I'd like to borrow for twenty-four hours." He pulled a credit card from his wallet. "Add $20,000.00 to my bill. When the books are returned, you can credit it to my account."

She shook her head. "I trust you to bring them back, Mr. Sterling. There's no charge."

"Thank you."

He put his credit card away and pulled out a hundred dollar bill. "You've been very helpful," he said, sliding it toward her. She started to make change but he told her not to bother.

"This is much too generous."

"Humor me, please," he said with a smile.

"If you insist. After all these years, it's so exciting to meet the legendary member of the Sterling family!"

Payne had heard that comment one too many times in his life. However it would do no good to remind the woman that his place in the scheme of things had happened because of an accident of birth. Her place had been determined the same way.

Furthermore, he got up in the mornings, worked hard, suffered, agonized and bled before going to bed at night, just the way she and everyone else did on the planet.

Her gaze searched his. "I do hope this turns out to be an honest mistake for all concerned."

"My sentiments exactly." Otherwise another nightmare had begun.

She bagged the books and handed the sack to him. He tucked *Manhattan Merger* inside the opening.

"I promise you'll get these back. Thanks again, Ms. Perry."

"You're welcome."

"Let's go," he murmured to Mac.

Once they were ensconced in the limousine, he phoned Drew Wallace, his attorney, and explained what had happened. They planned to meet at Crag's Head as soon as Drew could get away from an important dinner engagement.

Pleased Drew could come on such short notice no matter the hour, he told him he'd send the helicopter for him. This was one meeting that needed to take place tonight under strictest privacy.

When he returned to his sister's house, he discovered Diane in the backyard looking through some wedding magazines. Catherine was using doggie treats to make their family's golden retriever do tricks.

Though Payne loved all his nieces and nephews, he'd always had a special feeling for Catherine. Her heart melted for the less fortunates of this world whether they be animals or people.

Out of all his sister's children, Catherine was the one who'd taken her brother Trevor's death from leukemia the hardest. When she came into her inheritance, he had an idea she'd give it all to research in an effort to find a cure.

Since the shooting, his niece had attached herself to Diane, determined his brunette fiancée would walk again one day. Catherine's desire to make that happen had endeared her to Payne as nothing else could have done.

While Phyllis and Trent were away with their three older children, Payne's niece—who'd begged to stay behind—had been helping Diane and her mother with plans for their wedding. It was scheduled for August first.

Without Diane's knowledge Payne had already cleared his calendar so he could take Diane to Switzerland for the month. They would spend their honeymoon at a special hospital reputed to perform miracles on patients with Diane's type of injury. He was going to get her there no matter what.

After climbing out of the limousine, he handed Mac the sack before approaching his fiancée. Though her light brown eyes still looked haunted, she broke into a smile when she saw him.

He gave her a quick kiss on the lips knowing what he had to say would disappoint her, but it couldn't be helped.

"This problem with the romance cover needs to be dealt with. I'm afraid our plans to go into New York for dinner have to be put on hold."

"Somehow I knew you were going to say that."

"Drew's meeting me as soon as he can."

"That's good."

"After we've finished talking, I'll call you. In the meantime, Sam will run you home."

He pushed her wheelchair to the limousine, then lifted her into the back seat. Catherine and the dog ran over to say goodbye while John folded up the chair and put it in the trunk.

"Promise you'll phone later and tell me what's going on?"

He couldn't look at her in this condition without being

aware of her near lifeless legs. Though he might not have pulled the trigger, he was the reason she couldn't walk.

"You know I will." He gave her hand a squeeze, then shut the limo door.

"'Bye, Diane," Catherine called to her.

As the car drove off, Payne put an arm around his niece and walked her toward the house. He needed to get his laptop. "I want to thank you for being so good to Diane."

"I want her to get better."

"So do I." *So do I.*

"She's decided she'll never walk again, but I told her that's crazy because she still has feeling in her legs. I won't let her give up! Even if she doesn't want to go to that clinic in Switzerland, you have to take her, Uncle Payne."

He held the door open for her and the dog. Once they'd entered the house he said, "That's my plan."

"While you were in the village, she broke down crying and said she didn't want to go through another operation when it wouldn't do her any good."

Payne gritted his teeth. "I'm afraid seeing me on the cover of that book has brought back the horror of what she went through at Christmas."

"Then all the more reason for her to fight with everything she's got to get better!" Catherine blurted. "At least her doctor hasn't said her case is hopeless. It's not like what happened with Trevor," her voice wobbled.

"You're right." He kissed her forehead. "I love you for caring so much. When your mom asked me to look in on you while they were in Mexico, I was happy to do it. Tell you what— I'll free up some time tomorrow afternoon and take you and Diane sailing.''

''She doesn't like to sail.''

Payne had an idea something unpleasant had happened between Catherine and Diane. ''What's wrong, sweetheart?''

''Nothing,'' came the quiet response.

''You can say that to anyone but me.''

His niece looked up at him with soulful blue eyes. ''Diane got after me about reading romances. She said they're a waste of time and don't reflect real life.''

Until Payne had a chance to read *Manhattan Merger*, he would reserve judgment.

''You shouldn't take her disapproval to heart. She's a little down right now.''

''I'm not. She's been like this since you got engaged.''

His brows knit together. ''Like what?''

''Let's just say she has a hard time tolerating me when you're not around.''

''That's not true, Catherine. She cares for you enough to have wanted your help with our wedding plans.''

''She only asked me because you hinted it might be a good idea while mom and dad were away. I never told you this, but two years ago at that Fourth of July party on the yacht, Linda and I figured out Diane was in love with you when she told us to run along and leave you two alone.''

After what Catherine had just told him, he realized his perceptive niece understood a lot more about his fiancée than he'd given her credit for.

With so much on his mind at the time, Payne had been oblivious to Diane's interest in him. If he hadn't left his office that night... But all the what-ifs in the world weren't going to change the situation that had shattered lives and dreams.

After finding his laptop in the study he said, "Why don't you ask Linda to come sailing with us tomorrow, Diane or no Diane."

"Really?" Catherine's face broke into a sunny smile. "Thanks, Uncle Payne. You're the greatest!" She stood up on tiptoe to kiss his cheek. "I'll invite her when we get together later."

"You do that. See you later."

"Okay. Come on, Lady."

Before he left the house to join Mac in the other limo for the short drive ride to Crag's Head, he watched the dog follow her up the stairs. The Sterlings loved their animals. Payne was no exception, but after his bullmastiff Bruno had died, he'd decided not to get another dog.

Since moving into his new home, he was gone too much. It wouldn't be fair to keep a pet when he was away a lot of the time. They needed constant love and attention.

When he joined Mac in the limo he confided, "A few days ago I told Diane I missed having a dog and planned to get her one for a wedding present so she wouldn't be so lonely when I'm overseas. Apparently that's the last thing she wants, even though I pointed out it could serve as a guard dog too."

"It's not really surprising when you consider her mother's allergy to them," Mac murmured back. "Your fiancée didn't grow up around animals."

Payne rubbed the bridge of his nose. "Diane claims she's been in love with me for years, but since our engagement she's begun to realize how little we have in common. I'm afraid I'm not the perfect man she thought I was."

Mac eyed him frankly. "Don't hate me for saying this, but someone should have warned her about the old saying, 'Be careful what you pray for. You might get it.'"

"You're scary, Mac."

"How so?"

"You just took the words right out of my mouth. Last night she broke down and admitted she doesn't like my home." Mac grimaced. "Instead of a dog for a wedding present, could we build an English manor along the lines of her parents' home?

"I reminded her that as an only child she would inherit her family home one day, and could spend as much time as she wanted there after our marriage."

Mac didn't say anything. Neither did Payne.

After leaving his sister's sprawling New England style home which was reminiscent of many homes in the Hamptons, he craved his eyrie at Crag's Head.

Money could buy a lot of things he would never want, and it had brought him more pain than he'd ever thought possible. But if he could be grateful for one thing, it had allowed him to turn his ideas for the old lighthouse standing on family property into a sanctuary of primitive beauty and isolation.

Payne was an engineer, not an architect, but he'd known what he'd wanted the moment he'd glimpsed Le Corbusier's Chapel of Notre Dame Du Haut at Ronchamps for the first time.

Using a sculptural style rather than rectilinear, the famous French architect had created two curving walls of white-washed rough masonry that met beneath a dark roof.

Incorporating those same elements with the lighthouse, Payne's home stood like a piece of sculpture on the headland overlooking the Atlantic. The randomly punched out windows of the walls gave him all the privacy and all the view he could ever want.

He liked being able to walk around while he studied where he would lay massive fiber-optic cables in a place as difficult as New York's labyrinthine underground.

The urban fiber networks were one of the least-developed pieces of Internet infrastructure throughout the world. Payne had always considered it a market of vast potential.

Pleased to have been responsible for putting five million kilometers of glass thread in the ground already, he was now selling rights to individual strands of fiber outright. World carriers and corporations were coming to him every day asking for more.

When he'd had the place built, he hadn't yet met the woman he'd wanted to marry. If he'd given it any thought at all, he'd imagined that when the right one came along, she'd love it as much as he did.

Last night he'd promised Diane he would add some interior features to the second floor to make it less austere and fortress-like.

As for the lighthouse portion of his house, it had been transformed into an open workspace. It was here in his inner sanctum he used the thick rounded walls to spread out his huge maps of the tunneling beneath major American and European cities.

Considering he was in negotiations for the rights-of-way to dig in fifty more markets by next year, there was no way of gauging where it would lead in future years. But it ensured he wouldn't run out of problems to solve. That's what he loved to do.

That's why he was taking Diane to Switzerland, even if he had to drag her there. And if working with those doctors didn't produce a cure, he'd heard of another one who ran a clinic for injuries to the spine in Norway.

If Payne had already figured out how to unearth dazzling riches lying in mud beneath the streets of New York, Paris and Rome, surely he could find a way for Diane to walk again!

"Betty?" he called to Mrs. Myers. She and her husband lived in to look after his house and do light housekeeping. "I'm expecting Drew Wallace later tonight. When he gets here, let him in my study, will you please?"

"Of course. Would you like something to eat before he arrives?"

"How about a sandwich."

"Coming right up."

Taking advantage of the time, he sat back in his easy chair, adjusted the floor lamp light and began reading *Manhattan Merger*.

The opening line grabbed him by the throat.

Logan Townsend wasn't in love with his fiancée.

From that point on it was like walking through the minefield of his own psyche where his deepest thoughts and feelings were exposed at every unexpected turn. By the time he came to the last page and closed the book, his hands were literally shaking.

He recalled something Catherine had said before he'd left for Crag's Head.

Diane got after me about reading romances. She said they're a waste of time and don't reflect real life.

How wrong could Diane have been!

If Payne could be thankful for one thing, it was that Catherine hadn't read the story yet. It would bring her even more pain.

Once more the painting on the cover leaped out at him, underscoring his shock that this book with his picture was in circulation.

"Payne?"

At the sound of Drew's familiar voice, he levered himself from the chair. Only then did he realize he'd been too riveted to the well-written story to notice Betty had brought him a tray of food some time ago. Unfortunately his appetite had left him.

"I'm glad you're here."

"Good grief. You look like you've seen a ghost!"

"I wish that were the case. A ghost I could deal with," he muttered grimly.

Payne handed him the book. "I just finished reading it. No one, and I mean *no one,* could have reached down into my soul to pull things out the way this author did. I'm talking secret thoughts and feelings here."

His attorney took it from him and studied the cover. "There's no doubt about it. The person who did this artwork used a picture or photograph of you. Let's see the other books."

Payne emptied the sack onto his desk. Drew examined the covers of all the books.

When he eventually looked up he said, "Every day of life your picture appears somewhere in the newspapers or tabloids. The public has free access. That means you'll always be a target for unsolicited attention.

"But to find a painted picture of you on the cover of a book without your express written permission is a legal matter, never mind that the person responsible might or might not be a stalker."

"So you don't believe this could be a coincidence?"

Drew pursed his lips. "You have an aura that goes everywhere with you. Whoever did this painting caught your essence as well as the outer shell. I've a hunch this person has met you before, probably at your office."

Payne agreed, still haunted by the story. "I doubt the artist and the author are the same person, but I suppose it's possible," he theorized. "Regardless, something needs to be done right away. My niece and fiancée are terrified."

"With good reason," his attorney came back. "I admit I don't like this either." His thick brows met in a frown. "Rest assured I'll look into it first thing in the morning, then get back to you. I'll take these with me." He scooped up the books and put them in the sack.

"I promised the woman at the bookstore she'd get the four books back with my picture on them by Thursday at the latest."

"No problem."

Payne walked him to the north door which led to the pad where the helicopter was waiting. "Thanks for coming tonight."

"It was my pleasure. The sooner we find out if we need to call in the FBI, the better."

As he closed the door, Payne wasn't sure anything earthly could help. Not when the author knew things about him no one knew but God...

CHAPTER TWO

LORRAINE Bennett, known to most people as Rainey, had just set everything up to paint when her phone rang. It was only eight-twenty a.m.

Since she paid extra on her phone bill to avoid taking telemarketing calls, she figured it was Barbara Landers, one of the secretaries who worked for Mr. Goldberg, Rainey's boss at Global Greeting Cards.

Barb was the same age as Rainey, and single. They'd hit it off the first day they were introduced. Since then they'd often eaten lunch or dinner together.

Through Barbara, who was a native New Yorker, Rainey had met a lot of her friends at weekend parties. A couple of guys had already asked her to other parties and films.

Ken Granger, another guy who lived in her building and was clerking for a law firm, had taken her to dinner several times. Rainey's mother didn't need to worry that her daughter lacked for a social life.

Stepping away from the easel, she walked over to her desk and picked up the receiver.

"Rainey Bennett Fine Art Studio."

"Rainey? It's Don Felt again."

"Oh— Hi, Don!"

He was the head of the art department at Red Rose Romance Publishers. Only yesterday he'd phoned her about a new project, and had already faxed her the art-work sheets she needed to get started.

Between commissions from Global Greeting Cards and Red Rose, she had more work than she could handle at the moment. But of course she would never say no to a new project. This was her life and her livelihood!

"Sorry to bother you this early."

"This isn't early for me. I've already had my morning run in the park. What can I do for you?"

"Could you give me the name and phone number of the agency in Colorado you used for the male model on that sensational cover of *Manhattan Merger*?"

Her gaze clicked to the wall where she'd hung her oil paintings. Rainey was flattered that five out of the eight she'd done with him as the hero had already been sold to the authors who'd written the books featuring him on their covers. The ninth was in the beginning stages.

She had to admit those paintings *were* sensational even if she said so herself. However it was the *man* on the covers who made them so riveting. Rainey had only been the vessel to put him there.

"I didn't find him through a modeling agency, Don."

The artist in Rainey had been drawn to the face and body of a stranger whose rugged male beauty made her want to put him on every cover she did for Red Rose Romance.

It seemed the sales on those books had been phenomenal. The company had sent her red roses several times congratulating her for her excellent work.

Even better, the company had increased her salary to the point that she'd finally been able to move to New York and live on what she made doing artwork for them and the greeting card company.

"So—this masculine heartthrob who is setting hundreds of thousands of female hearts aflutter around the world is a figment of your imagination?"

"No." She sucked in her breath. "I'm afraid even my psyche couldn't dream up anyone that gorgeous."

"Then he must be a boyfriend you've been keeping secret from me."

She chuckled. "Don't I wish. To be honest, I have no idea who the man is."

After a slight pause, "Then how did you get permission to paint him?"

"I didn't. About two years ago I saw him in a photograph. His looks were so incredible, I found myself sketching him every time I went near my drawing board."

"Whose photograph?" he asked without preamble.

"My brother's."

"Do you still have it?"

"It was never mine to take. The only reason I happened to see it was because I was helping my mom clean his bedroom before he came home to go back to college.

"You know me and how I work. I often get ideas from people I see on the street or in a photo or some such thing. Later on if a face haunts me enough, I end up sketching it from memory.

"That's what happened in this case. A third of the covers I've painted for Red Rose have been done without models."

"I know, and there's never been any kind of problem. Maybe there isn't now."

She gripped the receiver a little tighter. "What's wrong, Don?"

"Possibly nothing. The legal department sent me a memo asking for the information."

She blinked. "Legal department... Do you know what this is about?"

"Not yet. But since you admit you saw this face in a photograph, humor me and talk to your brother."

"Don—you don't understand. The man in that picture was simply one of a group of vacationers. Craig is a whitewater river guide. Every summer he takes dozens of groups on float trips down the Colorado, and always gets a picture of them at the place where they put in.

"This is his sixth year. He must have close to a hundred group photos lying in a box in his bedroom closet. I have no idea how old that picture even was."

"Are they dated?"

"Probably. I wasn't paying any attention at the time. He plans to open up his own sporting goods store one day soon and use them for wall decor along with trophy fish and elk he's had mounted. He might remember something unique about a particular trip, but I doubt very much he could recall a name."

"Will you ask him anyway? Then get back to me with the information A.S.A.P.?"

"It's the end of June, Don. He's been running rivers for the last three weeks. All I can do is leave a message at Horsehead Whitewater Expeditions. That's the company Craig works for.

"They'll get word to my brother to call me, but it might take anywhere from a few days to a week before I hear from him."

There was another silence that increased her nervousness.

"Tell you what," Don murmured at last. "I'm going

to contact the legal department and find out why they're asking questions. Then I'll get back to you. Will you be there for a while?''

''Yes. I'm finishing up the painting for the cover of *The Bride's Not-So-White Secret*, and will send it over to your office by courier the day after tomorrow.''

''Excellent. I'll look forward to seeing it. Expect to hear from me soon.''

After they'd clicked off, she returned to the painting in question propped on her easel. Unfortunately the reason for Don's phone call had taken the zip out of her morning.

Instead of reaching for the brush to fill in the last bit of lace on the bridal gown, she walked over to the painting she'd done for *Manhattan Merger*.

There he was. The embodiment of her dreams come to life on a piece of canvas:

Rich dark brown hair that looked vibrant to the touch.

Nordic blue eyes that seemed to envision things no one else could even imagine.

Rugged facial features denoting a life of hard work, sacrifice and triumphs.

The build and stance of a conquerer beneath his business suit. Someone who dared to explore new frontiers.

A man who hadn't yet been transformed by a woman's love…

Perhaps because his total *persona* had enchanted her, she'd managed to breathe life into him. Enough life that she'd just been told this particular cover had taken first prize among all the covers on romance novels published by the various companies in the U.S. over the last twelve months.

The romance writing industry was going to present her with an award in August. Bonnie Wrigley, the author, would also receive an award for writing *Manhattan Merger,* chosen the best romance novel from the Touch of Romance line.

Much as Rainey was thrilled by this honor, she coveted this particular rendering of the man in the painting too much to part with it.

When Bonnie Wrigley had made inquiries to the art department for its purchase, Rainey had told Don it wasn't for sale. But she'd urged him to tell Ms. Wrigley that if it happened Rainey was the artist chosen to do another cover for her, she could have that painting for a minimal fee.

The phone rang again. Rainey rushed to answer it.

"Don?"

"No. It's Grace Carlow, the senior attorney in the legal department at Red Rose Publishing. I just got off the phone with Don and decided to call you myself."

Though the window air conditioner worked well, Rainey felt perspiration bead her forehead.

"Thanks for getting back to me so fast. I have to admit I'm a little anxious."

"After talking to Don, I think we're going to be all right. Where are you?"

"Near Eighty-Sixth Street and Lexington."

"That's good. Can you be at my office by ten?"

Rainey's green eyes widened. "You mean today?"

"Absolutely. The sooner we put out this fire, the better."

That didn't sound good.

"I'll explain when you get here. Come to the second floor. Make a left. I'm at the end of the hall."

The line went dead.

With heart pounding, Rainey showered and dressed in a straw colored wraparound skirt and pale blue cotton top. She brushed her gilt-blond hair which had been styled in a feather cut, slid on sandals and flew out the door of her furnished studio apartment.

There was no elevator, however the stairs were carpeted. She hurried down three flights to the entrance of the pre-World War II building, calling out hello to several people who lived there.

She'd been lucky to find a place this close to the Metropolitan Museum. Her rent might be horrible, and the landlord didn't allow pets which forced her to leave her dog behind with her parents. However this was a once in a lifetime opportunity.

If things didn't work out and her commissions fell off, she'd go back to Colorado. But she didn't anticipate that happening anytime soon.

So far the conversation with the attorney had sounded the only discordant note since she'd moved here four months ago.

After living in a small town all her life, she felt tiny walking between the skyscrapers. New York was like being in a different universe with every race and type of person represented. She loved the explosion of humanity amid the famous landmarks. Rainey loved the smells and sounds.

She loved Manhattan.

There was a pulse throbbing here. She was now a part of it. That's what made every day exciting.

Until today.

Since the phone call she'd had this awful pit in her stomach.

What if she'd done something so terrible, her happiness would be taken away?

Fear made her walk faster.

She entered Red Rose Publishers and took the stairs to the second floor. After reaching the end of the hall she entered the legal department and walked over to the front desk.

"I'm Lorraine Bennett. Grace Carlow is expecting me."

A young female receptionist told her to go on back to the first door on her left. Rainey complied.

"Good! You're on time." The attorney waved her inside. She was a tall, big-boned woman who was probably in her early sixties. She wore a white pantsuit with a black and white houndstooth print blouse. From the crown of her upswept blond hair she pulled down her glasses and studied Rainey for a moment.

"How old are you?"

"Twenty-seven."

"You don't look a day over twenty-one. Lucky you. Call me Grace." She smiled and extended her hand which Rainey shook. "Sit down."

Rainey took the chair opposite her desk. "I take it I've painted a celebrity by accident."

The woman made a funny noise in her throat. "Ever heard of the Sterling bank of America?"

She bit her lip. "Who hasn't?"

"Ever heard of Sterling Shipping lines?"

Rainey's body started to feel heavier in the chair. She nodded.

"Ever hear of U.S. Supreme Court Justice Richard Sterling?"

"Yes," Rainey whispered.

"Ever hear of Senator Phyllis Sterling-Boyce? Ambassador Lloyd Sterling? Rear Admiral Daniel Sterling?"

Her eyes closed tightly for a moment. "Of course."

By now Rainey was squirming.

Grace handed her a recent publication of *World Fortune Magazine.* "The whole lot of them don't even count compared to *this* Sterling."

Rainey took one look at the man on the cover and gasped.

King of Glass New York Billionaire-soon-to-be-Trillionaire Payne Sterling discovers ancient burial ground while mucking about with fiber-optic cable in his underworld kingdom close to Wall Street.

She read the caption twice before she studied the man in hard hat and jeans resting against an enormous cable.

Like pure revelation she understood why she'd been so drawn to him that she'd felt compelled to put his face and body to canvas.

"Oh boy." Rainey's voice shook before she handed the magazine back to Grace.

The attorney eyed her with compassion. "Oh boy is right. He's the embodiment of one of the sons of the Earl of Sterling who left England for America to build an empire of his own."

She tapped the cover. "This one shuns publicity like it was the plague of mankind, but he's so damned attractive it still comes after him, innocently or otherwise."

She winked at Rainey who groaned out loud.

"Cynthia Taft, the newest attorney to join our staff, handled *Manhattan Merger* while I was on a leave of absence. She came to us from Los Angeles and probably didn't catch the likeness because Payne Sterling is a celebrity in a very different pond than that of Hollywood.

"When I returned, I noticed his likeness on the cover and brought it to Claud's attention. However he said not to worry about it because there'd been no trouble with the other covers. What was done, was done, and this wouldn't be the first time an artist had unwittingly painted a cover that resembled a real person."

"Except that I did draw his face from memory," Rainey admitted.

"According to Don, you do that quite often."

"Yes."

"As I told you on the phone, I think we're going to be fine, but it will take the rest of the day to prepare our case."

Her pulse raced faster. "Case?"

"His attorney has already filed papers with the court. A judge is going to hold a closed door hearing tomorrow at two o'clock, so we have our work cut out."

"What?" Rainey cried out aghast. "You mean he's suing me?"

"You, the author Bonnie Wrigley and Red Rose Publishers."

"Good heavens—"

Grace's eyebrows lifted. "Don't forget you're dealing with a Sterling. The name moves mountains. But not to worry. He won't win.

"By the way, who's the person at Global Greeting

Cards who will give us an affidavit to the effect that you haven't put Mr. Sterling on any of their products?''

That was easy. "Saul Goldberg.''

She nodded. "I know Saul. Good man. All right. First things first. If we can get your mother and brother here in twenty-four hours, let's do it. Red Rose will be paying their expenses.''

"Mom could come. But I don't know if it's possible to reach my brother in time.''

Grace eyed her intently. "Try. Mr. Sterling's attorney, Drew Wallace, is the best there is if you know what I mean. He's pulled this in the hope of catching us unprepared, but we'll show him.''

Rainey admired the other woman's grit. Though she didn't know anything about Grace Carlow, she had an idea the attorney was actually enjoying this.

"I'll have to phone the company Craig works for and see if they can find him. My mother knows the number.''

"As long as you're phoning her, tell her to bring that photograph with her. One more thing. Don said you do preliminary sketches before you start your paintings. Where are your drawings of Mr. Sterling?''

She gave Grace a sheepish glance. "The old ones are stored at my parents' home.''

"Do you have pictures of them on disk?''

"No, only the finished portraits. Those disks are at my apartment.''

"I see. Tell your mother to bring the drawings too. When you get back to your apartment, burn the *new* ones!'' she fired.

Rainey could weep for the sketches she'd done of him

in cowboy gear as recently as three days ago. Sketches that would never appear on another book cover.

"Use my phone while I have a talk with Cynthia who's trying to track down Bonnie Wrigley. I'll be back in a minute to depose you."

As soon as Grace left the room, Rainey hurried around the desk to call home. It was only quarter after eight in Grand Junction. Her father was a dentist and had probably left for his office already. He would have to get his partner to cover for him so he could drive her mom to the Denver airport with the requested items.

Later in the year, after all his little patients were back in school, her folks had plans to fly out to New York. They were going to spend time taking in the sights, then rent a car and drive Rainey through New England to see the turning of the leaves.

As it stood, her mom, and possibly her brother, were going to get an unexpected sneak preview of New York from the inside of a courtroom.

"Good news," Grace announced ten minutes later. "Bonnie Wrigley will be at our office in the morning. How are things on your end?"

"Mom will fly in tonight with the items we need. The company Craig works for knows where he is and will get back to my father. Dad will call your office to let us know what's happening."

"Excellent. What do you want for lunch? They have great goulash and cheesecake at the deli down the street."

"That sounds good."

"Are you a coffee drinker?"

"No. Water or juice is fine."

She nodded before buzzing her secretary.

"All right." Grace sat forward with her fingers interlinked on top of the desk. "What Mr. Wallace will do is try to show that Red Rose Publishers willfully broke the law by using his client's likeness on the covers for monetary gain without obtaining his permission.

"He's asked us to bring the figures on the sales of those books to show that revenues went up when his client appeared on the covers."

"This is all my fault," Rainey whispered, feeling more and more ill by the moment. "He should be taking *me* to court, not the company."

"We're a family here at Red Rose. We defend our own, and we'll prove it was an honest mistake. The worst to happen will be that we're barred from using Mr. Sterling's likeness on any more covers.

"It's a shame, really," she added. "Though he's responsible for developing a whole new world-wide infrastructure, ninety-nine percent of our romance readership has no idea that Mr. Payne Sterling exists. All they care about is the man on those covers who is drop-dead gorgeous."

Rainey averted her eyes. "He is that."

"And you're the remarkable artist who brought him to breathtaking life. *Manhattan Merger* ranks among the ten bestselling novels ever put out at Red Rose. That speaks highly for you and Bonnie Wrigley who wrote the terrific story in the first place. Red Rose is lucky to have both of you on the team."

"Thank you. I hope you'll still be saying that when the hearing is over."

"I'm not worried. The truth will set us free, my dear. Why don't you start by telling me the process you went through from the moment Don phoned you about *Manhattan Merger* until you shipped off your painting to New York. Don't worry about dates. He has already supplied me with everything I need in that regard.''

Without preamble Rainey explained how she worked up a project. Grace interjected a question here and there. Lunch came and went. Still they talked. At three the phone rang through to Grace's office.

It was Rainey's father on the phone to tell her Craig's company had flown him to Las Vegas by helicopter and he would be arriving at JFK airport before midnight.

Grace's eyes lit up at that news. ''Your brother will be one of the key witnesses in your defense. I couldn't be more pleased to know he's coming. This is going even better than I expected.''

''If you say so,'' Rainey murmured.

''I do. Tomorrow morning we'll assemble here at eight-thirty in the conference room down the hall. I'll rehearse what's going to happen and prepare your mother and brother for the kinds of questions Mr. Wallace will ask during cross-examination. Your job will be to perform for Mr. Wallace.''

Rainey frowned. ''What do you mean?''

''I have a hunch he'll show you a picture of a man or woman you've never seen before, then ask you to sketch them from memory. He'll supply you with a sketch pad and pencils.''

''That won't be a problem.''

''Of course not.''

''What should I wear?''

''The outfit you have on is fine.''

Rainey got up from the chair. ''Thank you so much for your help. I'll never be able to pay you back.''

"This is part of my job."

"I'm still grateful to you. See you in the morning."

On the way back to her apartment, Rainey stopped to buy food and flowers before hurrying home to clean and get things ready for her family.

Her mother arrived by taxi at seven p.m., her brother at eleven. He'd come with his backpack and bed roll which turned out to be a blessing. Her mom could use the hide-a-bed and Rainey would sleep on the futon.

She would have given anything if their reunion could have happened under different circumstances. The idea that a New York billionaire was suing her and Red Rose Publishers was like her worst nightmare.

Before they all went to bed, Rainey sorted through the pile of photographs to find the one that had gotten her into so much trouble. When she finally came across it and showed it to her brother, he remembered the man, but not the name.

"What was he like, Craig?"

"He was in a group of twenty people. I do recall he was congenial, fascinated by everything and seemed totally at home on the water."

"Nothing else?"

"There is one thing that stood out," her brother murmured. "When I take people on a float trip, I mentally pick someone in the group I could count on to help in an emergency. He was the one I chose. Most people panic a little at some point on the river, but he never did."

After hearing Craig's testimonial, Rainey couldn't equate the man she'd painted with the person who could bring financial ruin to so many lives.

Grace had done her best to reassure Rainey things would be all right, but she had a hard time believing it. During the night she'd broken down sobbing. So, apparently, had Bonnie Wrigley who'd shown up in the conference room the next morning with drawn features and puffy eyes.

This was the first time they'd met each other. The minute the two women saw each other, they went out in the hall to commiserate in private.

At this point Rainey's guilt had increased a hundredfold. If it hadn't been for her cover, there would be no suit. Now poor Bonnie was going to have to explain how she dreamed up *Manhattan Merger,* where she got her ideas.

Before long Grace summoned them back to the conference room. The morning flew by while she coached everyone. After lunch was served, their entourage of twenty people left in taxis for the courthouse on Broadway.

When Rainey arrived with her family, it seemed to her there were an inordinate amount of security guards stationed outside the building. To her surprise, even more were positioned inside.

Several guards escorted her and her family to the designated courtroom where she saw more guards in place.

Though she might not be wearing handcuffs or leg chains, Rainey felt like a criminal. By the time they were seated down in front on the right side of the courtroom, she thought she would lose her lunch right there.

Grace came in with Cynthia Taft, the other attorney. They brought a look of calm as they took their places at the table in front of Rainey. Still she wasn't comforted. When she glanced at Bonnie, the other woman shook her head as if to say she couldn't believe this was happening.

Rainey couldn't fathom it either. There was an air of unreality about the entire situation.

Yesterday she'd gotten up motivated and happy, then received a phone call that had changed her whole life in an instant.

Immersed in pain, Rainey didn't notice the arrival of the opposition until Craig whispered to her.

She turned her head to see two men in dark business suits walking down the left aisle toward the table. Her gaze fell helplessly on the man from the photograph. The one whose looks and vitality had caught her artist's eye as no other man had done before.

He was tall and powerfully built, just as she'd remembered from the photograph. Yet he moved with careless male grace. It was one of those intangible traits you had to be born with.

The pool of genes that had come together to form the gorgeous man known as Payne Sterling was remarkable enough. When combined with the spirit that lived inside his body, he radiated a dynamism that made him much more attractive to her in person.

Afraid to be caught staring, she averted her eyes. It galled her to realize she could still be having these kinds of thoughts about him when he was the reason they were in court now.

"All rise."

Shocked to hear the bailiff's voice, Rainey lifted her head in time to see the judge enter the courtroom and take his seat.

"The court of New York County, New York, is now

in session. The Honorable James E. Faulkner, Supervising Judge of New York City, is presiding.

Supervising judge of New York? Rainey's legs trembled.

"You may be seated."

CHAPTER THREE

THE judge adjusted his glasses.

"The case of Sterling versus Red Rose Romance Publishers et al has come before the court in an emergency show causing hearing. All who testify will be sworn in.

"Mr. Drew Wallace, Counsel for the Plaintiff, will make opening remarks, followed by opening remarks from Ms. Grace Carlow, Chief Counsel for the Defendants."

Long ago Payne had learned the trick of staying focused. Never look at the opposition when inside the courtroom, but stare them down outside of it. That strategy had served him well in his business dealings. It would serve him even better in this particular circumstance.

The possibility that there might be a stalker within these walls never left his mind. After the experience of tackling that lunatic too late to protect Diane, he had no desire to look into the face of another psychotic woman with the potential to do harm.

This moment hadn't come soon enough for him or his family. He exchanged a private glance with Drew before his attorney got to his feet.

"Your Honor—Ms. Carlow—my client wouldn't have pushed for an emergency hearing without just cause. Six months ago he and his fiancée were entering his parents' home when a stalker shot at them. His fiancée is now in a wheelchair and may never walk again.

"Besides this tragic event, there have been half a dozen other stalking incidences in my client's past where police had to be called in and people arrested and prosecuted. It's all a matter of public record which I've submitted to the court.

"Two days ago my client discovered he was the man on the cover of a Red Rose Romance entitled *Manhattan Merger,* which I shall enter here in evidence as Exhibit One. The painting was done without his knowledge or permission." He handed it to the bailiff who took it to the judge.

"Apparently eight covers have been created with his likeness, all without his knowledge or permission. As you can see by the title of this particular story, it takes place in New York City. If you'll read the blurb on the back, it mentions a New York Billionaire who has an accident in the Canyonlands of the American West.

"In reading the novel, my client became alarmed by the amount of similarities to his life and that of the protagonist's.

"I have never been the victim of a stalker, but my client and his loved ones have already paid an enormous price because of the behavior of some crazed people in our society.

"My client has asked for a hearing to determine if this is a case of art imitating life to an uncanny degree, or if there is something more sinister behind so many incredible coincidences.

"Should today's hearing prove the latter, he wants this dealt with before anyone else gets hurt or killed. On that note I defer to Ms. Carlow.''

Payne gave Drew a satisfied nod.

"Your Honor, I speak for myself and everyone present when I say that we deeply regret Mr. Sterling's pain and suffering. The legal department at Red Rose Romance should have caught the problem when the first painting for *The Star Grazer* was shipped to our office.

"I noticed a likeness to Mr. Sterling in his facial structure and body type then, but the hero came from the future. He had red hair and brown eyes. I assumed it was a coincidence. It wouldn't be the first time a hero or heroine on one of our covers happened to resemble a real person.

"When the second painting of *Her Prince of Dreams* arrived, I again saw similarities though the hero had black eyes and black hair. However I still didn't feel concerned enough to say anything.

"It wasn't until Ms. Bennett had painted *Manhattan Merger,* that I could see the hero did indeed personify Mr. Payne Sterling. I believed it was because she'd placed him in a contemporary New York setting with the kinds of clothes a man in his position would wear to his corporate office.

"At this point I brought it to the head of the company's attention. Mr. Finauer said not to worry about it because there'd been no problem with the other covers.

"Though I can understand and sympathize with Mr. Sterling's alarm, as the attorney for Red Rose Romance Publishers, may I assure the court and Mr. Sterling that there is no stalker in this room as will be borne out in testimony.

"To save the court's time I've already supplied a list of witnesses in the order in which they will appear in this court. I've given the same list to Mr. Wallace, and have indicated home addresses, phone numbers and job descriptions.''

The judge nodded. ''Then this court will proceed. Ms. Farr, please take the witness stand.''

While the bailiff administered the oath, Payne could see that a sizable group from the opposition had assembled. Red Rose's attorney had come prepared. He would give them that much credit.

''Ms. Farr,'' Ms. Carlow began, ''state your full name and job description.''

''My name is Margaret Farr. I'm the head editor for the *Touch of Romance* line at Red Rose Publishers.''

''How long have you been at Red Rose?''

''Fifteen years.''

''Tell us about your relationship with Bonnie Wrigley, the author of *Manhattan Merger*. Give the court an idea of the process.''

''Bonnie's first manuscript came through the slush pile ten years ago. It was a wonderful book and I phoned her to tell her we were going to publish it. Since then she has written twenty-seven novels for us. *Manhattan Merger* was her twenty-fourth book. It was written for a promotion called 'Urban Tycoons.'''

Urban tycoons?

''Will you explain what you mean by a promotion?''

''Every month we put out six books in the *Touch of Romance* line. One or two of these books are usually part of a promotion or theme that has particular appeal for readers around the world. I made the suggestion to Bonnie that she write to the Urban Tycoon theme. She came up with *Manhattan Merger*.''

"Thank you, Ms. Farr. You can step down. I'd like to call Bonnie Wrigley to the stand."

To Payne's surprise the woman who was the next witness looked to be in her late fifties. Somehow he couldn't see her as a stalker, but he didn't suppose age mattered if a person were that unstable.

"Ms. Wrigley? Tell the court where you live."

"Spokane, Washington."

"Is writing a full-time career for you?"

"No. I'm a full-time Spanish teacher and write on the side."

"How long have you been a teacher?"

"Twenty-six years."

"How long have you been a writer?"

"Since I was twelve, but I didn't get published until ten years ago."

"Tell the court how you came up with your idea for *Manhattan Merger.*"

"When Margaret asked me if I'd like to write a book about a big tycoon, I decided he would have to be a billionaire because millionaires are too common these days.

"Since I'd already done several millionaire stories with European heroes who'd come from titled backgrounds, I thought I'd feature an American with ties to the English aristocracy. Someone whose family had amassed a fortune in real estate and shipping on the East Coast and had created a world bank.

"I decided he would have to be plagued by a problem that his billions couldn't fix.

"I thought, what if this billionaire has been diagnosed with leukemia? What if he decides to take a two week trip away from his fiancée and family to get his head on straight before he tells them what he found out during a routine physical exam? They think he's gone on another of his business ventures.

"As the blurb says, he has an accident in Canyonlands and is flown to a Las Vegas hospital where his secret is discovered by the attending physician who falls in love with him.

"I pictured her as a hardworking, dedicated young doctor who hasn't had time for men until now. Realizing the hero needs a bone marrow transplant, she asks everyone on the staff to give blood to find him a donor.

"When it turns out she could be a donor, the transplant takes place. It isn't until he returns to New York that he learns she helped save his life. When he confronts her, she tells him she did it because she loves him, but never wanted him to know because he's engaged to someone else.

"He confesses he was already in love with her before the transplant took place. As soon as he returned to New York, he broke off his engagement. Now he's proposing marriage. It's a Manhattan merger she can't turn down, not when they're joined body, blood and soul."

"Thank you, Ms. Wrigley. You can be seated. Mr. Felt? If you'll take the stand please."

While the third witness was sworn in, Payne leaned toward Drew. "When you cross-examine the author, ask her why she picked ties to the English aristocracy, how she happened to put in the part about archaeological sites. Why did she choose leukemia?"

Drew had already been making notes and nodded.

"Mr. Felt? How long have you been head of the art department at Red Rose Publishers?"

"Twelve years."

"Tell us what you do. Take us through the process when you handled *Manhattan Merger.*"

"As soon as a manuscript has been cleared for publication, the art department asks the author to fill out a form telling the theme of the book, the description of the hero and heroine, a short synopsis and a summary of several scenes that might look good on the cover.

"When we receive these sheets, we make a phone call to a freelance artist who does original oil paintings for Red Rose covers. We inform them we are sending information to help them create a painting that will sell books and please the author. We also send a printout of the manuscript for them to read.

"*Manhattan Merger* was handled like any other manuscript. I phoned one of our artists, Lorraine Bennett, about the project. She was free to go to contract on it. Our department sent her the filled out forms and the printout. She did the painting. When it was finished, she shipped it overnight courier to our office."

"Thank you, Mr. Felt. You can step down. Will Mr. Goldberg please take the stand?"

So far Payne hadn't heard anything to sway him either way. The artist was the person he wanted to tear apart with his bare hands. She would follow the next witness being sworn in.

"Mr. Goldberg?" Ms. Carlow began. "Tell the court where you work and what you do?"

"I'm the Vice President of Global Greeting Cards in New York."

"How long have you been with that company?"

"Nine years."

"Do all of your employees work in-house?"

"No we contract freelance writers and artists to produce the bulk of our inventory."

"Is Ms. Lorraine Bennett one of those artists?"

"Yes."

"Tell us the nature of her work."

"We send her the words, and she creates the art."

"Does she do portraits or people?"

"Neither. Her work is restricted to nature, flowers, wooded scenes, brooks and bridges, dogs and cats, that type of thing."

"How long has she worked for you?"

"Three years."

"Thank you, Mr. Goldberg. That will be all. Will Ms. Bennett please come to the stand?"

Payne answered some questions Drew had written down for him, then lifted his head. When he caught sight of the woman with the gilt-blond hair taking the oath, he felt a rush of adrenaline.

"I've seen that face before, Drew!"

"Where?"

He shook his dark head. "I don't know."

It was a fresh looking face. Wholesome. Attractive. So was the rest of her.

While he sat there staring at her, he racked his brain trying to remember.

"Ms. Bennett? Please tell the court where you live."

"In Manhattan."

"Have you always lived in New York?"

"No. I was born and raised in Grand Junction, Colorado. I only moved here four months ago."

Colorado—

Payne had once done some skiing there, but that was

years ago. If she'd only been in New York since February, then she'd done all the covers of him while she'd lived in Grand Junction.

So how in the hell did she know what his office looked like? He knew for a fact she hadn't been to his suite when he'd been there or he would have remembered.

"Did you ever visit New York City previous to moving here?"

"No."

"How long have you worked for Red Rose Romance?"

"Four years."

"We know you're employed by Global Greeting Cards too. Before you started freelancing, what did you do? Give us your background."

"I graduated from Colorado State University in Fort Collins, Colorado, with a B.F.A. in Art Education. That included an internship in Castiglion Fiorentino, Italy. After graduation I was hired to teach art at a high school in Grand Junction."

"How long did you teach?"

"Six years."

Ms. Bennett didn't look old enough to have been a teacher to a bunch of rowdy high school students for that long a time. Boys that age raged with hormones. With a woman so attractive and shapely, he could just imagine the drawings they'd generated of her. Drawings she would never know about.

"Will you tell the court how you prepare when you're doing a cover for a book?"

"As soon as the art sheet information arrives, I read

it carefully, particularly the theme. That's where all the emotion is centered. After that I read the novel and take a few days for the elements of the story to solidify in my mind. During that reflective period, I do research on the background details of the suggested scenes.

"Slowly the characters come to life for me. Sometimes I can picture him or her in my mind. When that happens, I start sketching like mad.

"Other times I study models from agencies until I see one that encapsulates my vision of the character in question. At that point I make an appointment for them to sit for me.

"Every day of life I see beautiful, interesting, fascinating faces in the crowd, in a photograph. Once in a while there will be a face that won't leave me alone.

"A certain bone structure, smooth olive skin, the lines of experience around a compelling mouth, piercing black eyes, the shape of an eyebrow black as a raven's wing— I find myself drawing this face weeks or even months later. Sometimes it ends up on the canvas."

"Tell us what happened when you painted the cover for *Manhattan Merger*."

Payne's gaze had been riveted on her classic features. There was a subtle change—a tension in her demeanor as soon as the attorney mentioned *Manhattan Merger*.

"The minute I read the novel, I knew who was going to be the male on the cover. I'd used him on seven other covers, but never as a contemporary American hero who is one of the powers that be in the corporate world.

"It was as if Bonnie Wrigley had written that novel with him in mind. Like the glass slipper that only fits Cinderella's foot, the melding of the right words and art can be a spiritual experience. That's how it was with *Manhattan Merger*."

"Did you use a model?"

"No. I'd seen the man in a photograph while I was helping my mother clean my brother's room."

"Did you know who he was?"

"No. But he had the spirit of a Renaissance man who could achieve anything. That's what was needed for the cover of this story to make it throb with poignancy. Imagine the reader falling in love with this extraordinary man so far ahead of his time, so endowed with superb male attributes, only to find out he's dying of a disease he's powerless to stop."

A stillness went out over the courtroom Payne could feel.

"Thank you, Ms. Bennett. You may be seated. If Mrs. Ellen Bennett will please come forward."

Drew turned his head, eyeing Payne with an enigmatic expression. His attorney wasn't the only one who'd been thrown a curve. Payne didn't know what in the hell to think.

"Mrs. Bennett? Please tell the court who you are and where you live."

"I'm Rainey's mother. My husband and I live in Grand Junction, Colorado."

"Do you work?"

"I'm a housewife, the hardest work I know."

Payne covered his face with his hand to hide his amusement.

"What does your husband do for a living?"

"He's a dentist."

"Do you have more than one child?"

"Yes. A son, Craig."

"How old is he?"

"Twenty-five."

"And your daughter?"

"Twenty-seven."

Twenty-seven—Payne couldn't believe it.

"You heard your daughter testify she saw a man in a photograph, the same man who ended up on the covers of eight romances. Will you please tell the court the circumstances of that day?"

"Yes. Rainey had come over to the house from her apartment to help me spring houseclean Craig's bedroom. He's a packrat. While we were cleaning under his bed and straightening his closet, we found boxes of his memorabilia. Frankly, everything was in a mess.

"We decided to separate his belongings into piles and put them in separate baskets that could be stacked. Rainey found the photographs he'd been collecting over the years of his river running experiences."

The Colorado River—

Was that where Payne had seen her face?

"As she was placing them in one of the baskets she said, 'Oh mom—you've got to see the incredible man in this photograph!'

"I looked where she was pointing and had to admit he really was something. But knowing my daughter, I realized she was struck by things beneath the surface too. That's what makes her such a remarkable artist.

"She studied the picture a little longer, then put it away with all the other pictures. I never heard her mention him again. To my knowledge, she never went near Craig's closet again. In truth, neither of us would want to!"

In spite of the seriousness of the situation, Payne chuckled at the remark. He glanced at Drew. The other's man lips were twitching.

"Thank you, Mrs. Bennett. You may be seated. We have one more witness, Your Honor. Will Mr. Bennett please come to the stand?"

The blond Colorado River guide who'd shown Payne such a fantastic time two summers ago was the last person he expected to see in this courtroom. But there he was, bigger than life, reaching the witness stand in a few athletic strides.

When he turned around, Payne found himself looking at the male version of Ms. Rainey Bennett. Now he had his answer. Payne couldn't imagine a better looking brother and sister.

Unfortunately Craig Bennett's appealing white smile was missing. Dressed in a suit rather than cutoffs and T-shirt, he looked older, less approachable as he took the oath and sat down.

"Mr. Bennett? Please tell the court where you live, what you do for a living."

"When I'm in Grand Junction I live with my parents. During the summers I live in Las Vegas or on the Colorado River where I work for Horsehead Whitewater Expeditions."

"Tell the court the nature of your work."

"I'm a river guide for people who want to take a float trip down the Colorado River."

"How many trips do you take a summer?"

"Dozens."

"Does this involve individuals or groups of people?"

"I take as few as four, or as many as twenty at a time."

"Do you see anyone in this courtroom who has taken a trip down the Colorado with you?"

"Yes. My mom, my sister and the man sitting over there." He nodded in Payne's direction.

"Do you know his name?"

"I do now. At the time he used another name which I don't recall. Something like Vince or Vance."

"Vince," Payne whispered to Drew.

"Do you remember taking a picture of him?"

"I always snap a photo of my group where we put in the river."

"Your Honor?" Ms. Carlow interjected. "I have that picture with me and would like to enter it in evidence as Exhibit Two."

Payne watched the bailiff hand it to the judge. He studied it for a moment.

"Mr. Bennett?" opposing counsel continued. "Did you ever discuss this man with your sister?"

"Never."

"Did she ever bring him up to you?"

"No."

"Did you know she was making sketches of him from memory?"

"No."

"Have you ever read any of the romance novels with her paintings on the covers?"

"I would never read a romance novel period."

Strike two against the male of the species.

"Thank you, Mr. Bennett. You may step down. That's all I have to present at this time, Your Honor."

The judge's gaze swerved to Drew. "Mr. Wallace? Do you wish to cross-examine?"

"I do, Your Honor."

"May I remind the witnesses you are all still under oath. Go ahead, Mr. Wallace."

"If Ms. Wrigley will come forward again please?" As soon as the older woman took her place he said, "How many times have you visited New York City?"

"This is my first time."

"My client is curious to know why you picked English royalty, why the East Coast, why banking?"

"I'm a genealogist. I've researched most of my ancestors who came from England. They were all as poor as church mice. However when you dig back in those old English lines, you come across fascinating information about the families who descended from kings, lords, earls and the like to build new fortunes in America.

"Every time I come across information like that, I keep it in a special research file for my writing. Most of the wealthy arrivals had banking and shipping interests. Upon reaching our shores, it was common for them to buy large tracts of land on the East Coast."

"I see," Drew murmured. "When you filled out the art sheet, did you suggest Ms. Bennett put the picture of a ship and lighthouse on the wall of the hero's office?"

"No."

"What about the dog in the picture?"

"No."

"Will you explain why you inserted a scene in your book where the hero comes across an ancient burial ground and has it designated as an official archaeological site?''

"Yes. When Frontenac came to the Eastern seaboard on an exploration expedition for the King of France, he discovered this was a land filled with the bones of hundreds of thousands of men, women and children who'd died in great battles of extinction long before the white man came here.

"The State of New York is really one massive burial ground. Every so often a farmer is digging in a field and finds the remains of bodies thrown in haphazard piles, the points of their weapons of war still embedded in their bones.

"In *Manhattan Merger* my hero heads a corporation that develops land, but he's a man who respects the first inhabitants of this land. That's why I have him heading a foundation for the preservation of all ancient artifacts, mounds, burial grounds, observatories found in New York.''

"Did you know of the name Payne Sterling when you wrote your novel?''

"I had no knowledge of his name or existence until yesterday when I received a phone call from the company attorney, Ms. Carlow.''

"One last question. Why leukemia?''

"Years ago our daughter died of leukemia. That was something my husband and I couldn't fix. It was the first thing that came to my mind when I was considering what kind of illness to give my hero.''

"Thank you, Mrs. Wrigley. You may be seated. If Ms. Bennett will please take the stand one more time.''

While Payne sat there mulling over Ms. Wrigley's answers, the adorable looking artist whose figure transformed the skirt and blouse she was wearing, walked to the front of the courtroom and sat down.

"Ms. Bennett? You've done seven other covers with this man's picture. Why is that?"

"Red Rose Romance has nine lines of books. Each line has a different readership. Of course there are crossovers, meaning people who read more than one line.

"If a certain face is popular, it is used more than once because it sells more books. Every time this man's face appeared on a cover, the sales climbed, so I was asked to do more pictures. I've been told *Manhattan Merger* is the biggest seller to date."

"How did you happen to put a ship on the wall of the hero's office?"

"It seemed logical that a man whose ancestors crossed the ocean and built a shipping empire would have such a picture to remind him of his heritage and his love of the sea."

"How did you happen to paint that particular ship?"

"I did research to find the right kind of vessel for the time period Ms. Wrigley mentioned in the book."

"Why the lighthouse too?"

"One of my favorite living artists is Thomas McKnight. He did a surrealistic painting of a lighthouse on Nantucket. I adore that painting."

Payne happened to love that painting too.

"While I was working on the cover for *Manhattan Merger,* a lighthouse just sort of slipped in there while I was painting the ship."

"Explain the reason you put a dog in the picture on his desk."

"In Ms. Wrigley's novel, there's a part where the hero

has just found out he's dying of leukemia. Memories of his past life flash through his mind. One of them is running along the beach with his dog when he was a boy.

"This hero is a loner by nature. Obviously his dog meant a great deal to him. That's why I painted it in."

"Did Ms. Wrigley mention the breed?"

"No."

"Then why a bulldog?"

"For years I've had an English bulldog named Winston, after Winston Churchill, my favorite figure in history. At present the dog is staying with my parents until I can find a place that will allow pets.

"While I was doing the painting for *Manhattan Merger,* Winston happened to be sitting on one of the kitchen chairs watching me. He was so darling, I put him in the picture without even thinking about it."

Incredible. Absolutely incredible. Payne could only shake his head.

"Ms. Bennett, you testified that you'd never been to New York before you moved here. You also testified you went to school in Italy. Did your flight involve a stop in New York?"

"No. I took a nonstop charter from Denver to Frankfurt, Germany, and from Germany back to Denver when school was over. You can contact the art department at Colorado State to verify everything."

"Thank you. Will you tell the court the location of the eight paintings with my client's likeness?"

"Five of the authors have bought the paintings from me. I own the other three, one of which is *Manhattan Merger.* They're hanging in my apartment."

"According to the testimony we've heard, you only

saw my client in a photograph for a few minutes, then painted him from memory.''

"Yes.''

"If Your Honor will permit, I'll ask the bailiff to give this sketch pad and pencil to the witness.''

The judge nodded.

"Now if Your Honor will assist me by picking another person in the photograph from Exhibit Two? Show it to the witness. Let her study it for a moment, then ask her to draw this person from memory.''

Payne whispered an aside to Drew. "If Ms. Bennett can pull this off, then we have no stalking case, thank God.''

"Amen,'' Drew muttered.

First five, then ten minutes went by while the room sat in frozen silence waiting for her to finish her drawing. Payne watched her face and body change expression several times. Her concentration was almost as disarming as her femininity.

Finally she looked over at the judge and rendered him the sketchbook. He studied it and compared it to the photograph.

"You not only have a photographic memory, Ms. Bennett, you're a very gifted artist.''

"Thank you.''

"You may step down.''

He signaled the bailiff to take the sketch and photograph to Drew. An impatient Payne was forced to wait until he could examine both items for himself.

"Good grief—'' he blurted when Drew moved aside. "It's Mac— She's done a perfect likeness of him!''

"Her talent is remarkable.'' Drew turned to the judge.

"I have no more questions of these witnesses, Your Honor."

"Ms. Carlow? Do you wish to make your closing remarks now?"

"Yes, Your Honor. I believe the facts speak for themselves. In future, Red Rose Publishing will require every artist to use licensed models for their covers. Needless to say, Mr. Sterling's likeness will never appear on another cover of a Red Rose Romance.

"I instructed Ms. Bennett to bring all drawings and disks with Mr. Sterling's likeness to this court. They can be turned over to him, or Red Rose can destroy them. Whatever the court wishes.

"It's worth noting that the cover of *Manhattan Merger* won first prize out of all the romance covers printed in the United States within the last twelve months.

"Ms. Wrigley also won first prize for the best *Touch of Romance* novel for *Manhattan Merger*. Both women were going to be honored at a banquet this fall.

"Under the circumstances they'll forego those awards in order to spare Mr. Sterling any unnecessary publicity or exposure. Our company will instruct the people at the U.S. Romance Author/Publisher Convention to pick two other winners.

"As for the books already in print and shipped out through the book club, it would be impossible to judge how many readers would know the man on the cover is Mr. Payne Sterling.

"Your Honor?" she said after taking a drink of water. "Would it be permissible to ask how Mr. Sterling came to find out his likeness was on the cover of *Manhattan Merger*?"

The judge looked at Drew. "Mr. Wallace?" he prompted.

Payne nodded when Drew turned to him for permission.

"His sister's daughter reads romances and noticed the likeness. So did the maid who's also a romance reader."

Ms. Carlow smiled. "Thank you, Your Honor."

"Is there anything else, Counselor?"

"No."

"Very well." The judge looked at Drew. "Mr. Wallace? Are you ready to make closing remarks?"

"Yes, Your Honor. The extensive amount of testimony provided by the defendants has ruled out any hint of stalking violations which was my client's primary fear.

"My client could wish the published books with his likeness on the covers weren't in the public domain. However in view of Ms. Carlow's assertion that my client's likeness will never again grace a future Red Rose Romance cover, another fear has been removed.

"At this time my client and I would like to thank the court for hearing this case in such a timely manner. I also wish to congratulate opposing counsel for the outstanding defense she prepared on such short notice."

After Drew sat down, the judge removed his glasses. "I too want to compliment both parties for conducting yourselves in a professional manner. This is an unusual case to come before the court."

Payne suddenly heard a voice cry out from the other side of the room.

"Your Honor?"

"Yes, Ms. Bennett?"

"Could I say something?"

"Go ahead."

"If I had been Mr. Sterling, I would have brought this case to court just as he did in the hope of preventing another tragedy. But Red Rose Publishing is not to blame. Neither is Bonnie Wrigley.

"I—I'm the one who painted him without permission and brought him more grief unknowingly," her voice trembled. "Ignorance is no excuse. I'm the guilty party. I feel so horrible about it, I don't know how to begin to make restitution.

"If there's to be a severe financial punishment, let it be on my head, no one else's."

"Thank you, Ms. Bennett. I do believe you've learned an important and necessary lesson in the early stages of your brilliant career. You never know who the stranger in the crowd or the photograph might turn out to be.

"A priceless gift like yours is going to have to be used with care in the future, as you've discovered. Call it destiny or fate, you happened to paint the one man whose phenomenal success in life has made him vulnerable to the ugliest elements in our society. The tragedy that befell his fiancée should never have happened.

"It is also unfortunate that no one at Red Rose Publishers caught the problem in time to rectify it. However Ms. Carlow has assured the court that the company will require its artists to use licensed models from now on. A very wise move which will prevent unwanted occurrences like this from happening again.

"As for Ms. Wrigley's scholarly researched fiction novel which paralleled Mr. Sterling's life to a great degree, testimony has proved it to be one of those inexplicable coincidences. Counsel for the plaintiff said it best. 'Art imitating life.'

"In conclusion, the court has listened to testimony and finds no evidence of evil doing or intent to do evil on the part of Ms. Bennett, Ms. Wrigley or Red Rose Romance Publishers.

"Opposing counsels can get together to decide on disposition of drawings, disks, paintings, books already in print that can still be pulled, books that are still awaiting translation for foreign markets, et cetera."

The judge pounded his gavel. "Case dismissed."

CHAPTER FOUR

THE second the judge left the courtroom, Rainey was so relieved she leaped from the chair to hug Grace Carlow. The attorney dwarfed her five foot six inch body.

"It turned out as I knew it would, my dear."

"Only because of you," Rainey half sobbed the words. Relief swept over her in waves.

"Rainey's right," Bonnie chimed in, giving both of them a hug. "Without your confidence, I would have had a coronary before we ever got off the phone."

Grace smiled. "It's over, and the lesson we've learned has been instructive for the company."

Rainey nodded.

"We also learned something else, ladies." She cocked an expressive brow.

"What?" Rainey and Bonnie were both wiping their eyes at the same time.

"Mr. Sterling only has one sister. It means Senator Sterling-Boyce's daughter and maid read our romances. That's the kind of inside information guaranteed to make Mr. Finauer's day."

Rainey had never met the CEO, but she'd heard that when he erupted, everyone felt the shock waves. If this case had gone the wrong way...

"All's well that ends well, honey."

"Oh, mom—" Rainey turned to embrace her mother and brother. "Thanks for flying to my rescue on such short notice and bringing everything. The outcome would have been very different without you two!''

Craig gave her a hug. ''Congratulations on your big honor, even if you can't accept the award.''

''Thanks.''

''Trust my sister to pick the *one* billionaire face in the crowd,'' he teased.

She groaned, still shuddering from nerves which had been playing havoc with her emotions over the last twenty-four hours.

Her brother grinned. ''I guess I'm going to have to break down and read *Manhattan Merger* to find out why Mr. Megabucks felt so violated.''

''We'll never know all the things about Bonnie's novel that upset him so much. But it wouldn't hurt you to read a really fantastic relationship book with a powerful emotional punch.'' Rainey sniffed. ''Maybe it will give you insight into your less than satisfactory love-life.''

''How come it hasn't helped yours?'' he whispered.

''It has! Reading romance novels has taught me to wait for the kind of man I want for my husband. He just hasn't come along yet.''

''Ms. Bennett?'' a deep unfamiliar male voice sounded behind her.

She whirled around, but felt like she was still reeling after she'd come to a stop.

The man she'd drawn, painted and dreamed about so many times was actually standing in front of her, up close and too personal for her to breathe normally.

With a sense of déjà vu her gaze traveled over his rugged male features. There were strain lines near his eyes and mouth that hadn't been there two years ago. Lines put there by a stalker who'd crippled this man's fiancée...

No doubt those creases had deepened further as a result of finding himself on the cover of *Manhattan Merger,* a book that paralleled his life to such a degree, he'd not only felt violated as Craig had said, he'd felt threatened.

"I would give anything if I could undo the pain and suffering I've caused you and your fiancée—" she blurted. Her smoky green eyes glistened with tears that trembled on the tips of her velvety black lashes.

"Please tell her how sorry I am to have been the person who turned your lives into another nightmare. I can't even imagine how terrible that experience must have been for both of you and your families."

"It was. I won't lie to you about that."

His honesty was as devastating as his dark blue gaze which traveled over her features with an intimacy that made her tremble.

She averted her eyes. "It's a helpless feeling to know you've done something you can't undo—like trying to recapture the air from a balloon. If I could turn the clock back, knowing what I know now—" she half moaned the words.

"Amen," he muttered with an unmistakable echo of pain revealed in that one word. It haunted her. "My attorney will be calling Ms. Carlow about the paintings of me still in your possession."

She nodded. "Naturally you'll want proof that everything has been destroyed."

"Excuse me for interrupting, Ms. Bennett," his attorney broke in on them. "I need to talk to my client."

"Of course." Her eyes lifted to Payne Sterling's once more. "Thank you for not pressing charges against the others...or me. I'll always be grateful," her voice throbbed. "God bless you and your fiancée."

She turned away from him, feeling much worse than before because he was no longer just a memory from a photograph. The reality of his physical presence, plus the pain she felt emanating from him, had combined to squeeze her heart with fresh guilt.

"What did he say to upset you?" Craig whispered as he and their mother walked her out of the courtroom.

"Nothing. I just feel horrible for causing him and his family more pain."

"It wasn't intentional and he knows it," her mother assured her. "Let's be glad it's over. Since Craig and I have to fly back home in the morning, shall we celebrate your victory and take a ferry to Staten Island if it isn't too late? It's something I've always wanted to do."

"That sounds like a good idea, mom." Anything to get her mind off of Payne Sterling for a while. "We'll grab a taxi out in front of the court building and head for the terminal. If I remember right, the ferries leave often during rush hour."

"When we get back, I'll treat us to dinner," her brother offered. "Where shall we go?"

"There's a great sushi place on Bond Street." She'd said it to tease Craig. His proclivity for beef was well known.

When both he and her mother frowned on cue, Rainey laughed. "Just kidding. I'll take you guys to Del Frisco's. It's the best steak house in Manhattan."

"Now you're talking."

They moved outside the building to hail a cab. "I'm surely glad you've lived around here long enough to know your way around, Rainey," her mother confided. "You love it, don't you."

"On the whole, yes. But the masses of people can be daunting at times. To live here permanently would require a lot of money if you craved isolation and privacy."

"Luckily we have that for free in Grand Junction," Craig said before letting out an ear-piercing whistle. It did the job. One of the taxis whizzing by came to a quick stop.

Rainey climbed in after her mother. Then Craig got inside and pulled the door closed after him.

She leaned forward to address the driver. "Whitehall Terminal, please."

As the taxi started up again, Rainey noticed Payne Sterling and his attorney, both in sunglasses, leave the courthouse surrounded by a group of men all in business suits. They got in a limousine with tinted windows.

After the accident that had left his fiancée paralyzed, Rainey imagined he would always be well guarded. How horrible to be a target everywhere he went. She shuddered.

Her brother eyed her with concern. "Are you all right?"

"I'm thankful he didn't press charges, but I still feel awful about what I did."

"As the judge said, there was no evil intended. Chalk it up to one of your exciting experiences in the Big Apple. Someday you'll look back and laugh about it."

"I hope so."

"Craig's right, honey. I'm sure Mr. Sterling's relief

that neither you or Bonnie Wrigley was a stalker has caused him to forget about it already.''

''Even if that's true, he has to live every moment of his life with the knowledge that his fiancée is in a wheelchair because of a demented woman who imagines herself in love with him.''

''That's the downside of being a man with a name like Sterling, and a bank account that could fund the homeless forever.''

Rainey bowed her head. ''Grace told me he already does that.''

''Does what?'' her brother asked.

''He's a philanthropist. According to her he has set up many charities including a foundation for the homeless. I know he does it for tax purposes, but I'm pretty sure she told me all those things to reassure me he's compassionate too.''

''He seemed like a good man to me when I took him rafting down the river. No wonder he used the name Vince. It's the only way he can have any anonymity.''

She buried her face in her hands. ''I still can't believe I picked him to paint.''

''I can,'' her mother drawled. ''So can all the millions of women who will mourn when he's not on any more romance covers.''

''Mom—'' Craig laughed. ''I can't believe you just said that.''

''You'd have to be a woman to understand.''

''Is dad aware of your secret fantasy?'' he teased.

''There are several things he's better off not knowing.''

''Don't tell me you read those romances too?''

"Rainey and I have been enjoying them for years. You were always too busy devouring your hunting and fishing magazines to notice."

At this point Rainey couldn't help chuckling. Her mother's comments had managed to lighten her mood.

"It looks like we've arrived," Craig muttered, sounding miffed by their mother's confession.

On the whole Rainey found that men seemed uncomfortable by the thought of romance novels and heroes. It was very strange since statistics showed that men had fantasies about women on a daily basis.

Rainey lifted her head in time to see her brother pay the fare. They piled out of the taxi into a horde of people coming and going from the ferry. It happened to be the *John F. Kennedy.*

Craig pulled out his pocket camera and snapped a picture, then herded them toward the terminal for their tickets.

Being with her family until they left for the airport the next morning prevented Rainey from dwelling on the whole disturbing incident with Mr. Sterling. Her long talk into the night with Craig about his business plans had kept disturbing thoughts of him at bay.

But once she'd waved them off in a taxi headed for the airport, memories of him came rushing back with a vengeance.

To stem the tide, she straightened her apartment, did a wash and scoured the bathroom. When everything was neat and clean, she showered and dressed in cutoffs and a T-shirt. After going downstairs for her mail, she was ready to get back to her painting.

An hour later she'd finished the lace on the wedding

gown. The cover for *The Bride's Not-So-White Secret* was done.

She called the courier service to schedule a pickup for Monday morning. Now she could start on the next project for Global Greeting Cards which had come in the mail.

No sooner had she put the receiver back on the hook to get busy and her phone rang. She assumed it was Ken. He'd asked her to go to a jazz concert with him tonight in Greenwich Village and was probably calling to set up the time.

"Rainey Bennett Fine Art Studio."

"Hello, Rainey."

"Grace—" She clutched the receiver a little tighter for fear something else was wrong.

"Relax, my dear. All is well. Claud Finauer couldn't be happier with the outcome."

Relieved to hear that news, Rainey let go of the breath she'd been holding.

"For your information I had a call from Mr. Wallace a few minutes ago. If it's convenient, someone will be coming by your apartment within the hour for your paintings of Mr. Sterling. I wanted to make certain you were home."

"I'll be here. Tell them to buzz me from the foyer so I can let them in. I'm on the third floor."

"Good. I'll call you next week. We'll go out for lunch."

"I'd like that." Grace was a fascinating personality.

"So would I. Talk to you soon."

The minute they clicked off, Rainey walked over to

the paintings and removed them from the wall. After dusting the frames off, she placed them next to the door.

It was a wrench to have to give up the one for *Manhattan Merger*. Not that she couldn't do another painting of him from memory. But it would be different the second time around because she'd seen him in person.

If she did do any new sketches, they would show a man embracing his wheelchair-bound fiancée. His eyes and rugged features would reveal intense suffering...

While she waited for the runner from Mr. Wallace's law firm to arrive, Rainey opened the manilla envelope. It appeared she was to design a series of cards that said "Goodbye—Enjoy your trip!" in various languages.

Having lived in Italy, she reached for her sketch pad and began playing around with some ideas that immediately sprang to mind. Soon her hillside in Tuscany began to come alive like the pieces of a patchwork quilt.

She drew in one of those charming farmhouses with the tiled roof. No one could see inside it, but her imagination allowed her to dream of two people madly in love. They stood at one of the windows overlooking their own spot of heaven. Twilight revealed two bodies entwined.

As Rainey stared into space, she realized she'd been envisioning herself in Payne Sterling's arms. It wasn't the first time this had happened. She feared it wouldn't be the last.

Disturbed by thoughts she had no right to entertain, she threw down her pencil and got up from the desk.

It was a good thing all physical evidence of him would be gone in a few minutes.

But not from her mind.

An overwhelming compulsion to look at him one more time drove her to the door of her apartment. She reached for her favorite painting.

The more she studied it, the more she realized the person who'd gone down the Colorado with her brother seeking adventure bore little resemblence to the man she'd faced in the courtroom.

Rainey finally put it back with the others.

How tragic to think the woman he'd fallen in love with could no longer run into his arms. Talk about cruel.

She tried to imagine herself in his fiancée's place. How hard it must be for her to want to do everything for him, to share everything with him when she—

The buzzer sounded from the foyer, interrupting her tormented thoughts. She spoke through the intercom. When she'd ascertained it was the runner, she told him to come up.

A half minute later there was a rap on the door. She opened it expecting to see a college-age person. Her greeting stuck in her throat to find a huskily built man blocking her exit. He was in his late thirties and wore casual clothes.

"Ms. Bennett?"

"Yes?"

He looked beyond her to the apartment itself, as if he were casing the interior. Sensing something wasn't right, she was about to close the door when another man came up behind him dressed in a business suit.

"I'll take it from here, John."

The second Rainey saw who it was, the breath rushed out of her lungs. Maybe she was hallucinating.

The all-seeing blue eyes of Payne Sterling seemed to

take in every detail of her face and body before their gazes locked.

"I'm here for the artwork, Ms. Bennett, but I'd like to talk to you first." His cultivated male voice permeated her bones. "May I come in?"

Rainey couldn't believe this was happening. Thank heaven she'd done her housecleaning earlier that morning.

"Yes. Of course."

Once he'd stepped inside and shut the door, he dominated her tiny studio apartment.

"Would you like to sit down?" Even to her own ears she sounded breathless.

His glance darted to the sketch on her desk. "I can see that I've interrupted your work, but I don't plan to be here that long. I've come to ask a special favor of you."

Rainey gulped. "If you're worried about the other paintings, I'll phone those authors who purchased them. When they hear what happened, they'll send them back to me."

He shook his dark head. "Forget them. My concern lies in making my niece and fiancée feel secure. They're the ones who panicked when they saw my likeness on the cover."

His hands went to his hips, underscoring his compelling masculinity. "I'd like them to meet the artist. Between you and me, I'm confident we'll be able to dispel their fears that you're a threat to me or anyone else."

She was stunned by his request.

For one thing, she'd never imagined seeing him again. For another, it brought home the fact that she'd unwittingly terrorized two innocent people who loved him and needed reassurance.

No matter his reasons for asking this favor of her, somewhere in Rainey's psyche she knew she should say no for her own self-preservation.

What was it she remembered about the cycle of temptation?

First you allowed the thought to enter your mind. Then you began to fantasize about it. From there you started making plans. Finally you found yourself acting on those plans.

The man she now knew as Payne Sterling had been in her thoughts for two years. Since court she'd entertained certain intimate fantasies about him. If she agreed to his request, it meant crossing that precarious line into the ''making plans'' phase.

What really shocked her was how much she wanted to make plans with him, even though it meant meeting his fiancée. Was she some kind of masochist?

Clinging to one last thread of common sense she said, ''They're welcome to come here to my studio.''

''It would be easier for my fiancée if I take you to them.''

Of course. The apartment didn't have an elevator. What was the matter with her?

''I'd like to surprise them with good news,'' he continued. ''It'll be the best medicine of all.''

But not for me Rainey's heart cried. Help—what should she do?

''When were you thinking of us meeting?'' She fought to keep the tremor out of her voice.

"As soon as possible. Perhaps this evening after we've both finished work for the day."

This evening?

A shiver of excitement passed through her body.

"I see." She bit her lip remembering it was Friday and she had a date with Ken.

"By your hesitation I assume you're not free."

His eyes held hers. She could sense his urgency and the accompanying disappointment.

"I—I'll change my plans," she stammered. "After the pain I've put you and your family through, it's the least I can do."

Ken would forgive her when she told him it was a legal matter. He above all people would understand.

The only person who didn't feel right about the whole situation was Rainey. Not when her attraction to this man was so intense.

"Thank you, Ms. Bennett. Have you ever flown in a helicopter?"

Her pulse started to race. "Yes. My brother's friend runs a helicopter service in Las Vegas. He's flown me over the Grand Canyon several times."

"Good. I'll send the limo for you at four o'clock. We'll leave from my office as soon as you arrive. Do you have plans for tomorrow?"

"Work—" she blurted, throwing herself a lifeline. "I'm behind becau—"

"Because I forced you into court," he finished for her. "Bring it with you and anything else you'll require for an overnight stay, including a bathing suit."

Oh no.

Rainey averted her eyes. She was terrified he would see how excited she was at the prospect of going anywhere with him...of spending time with him.

And his fiancée, a little voice nagged. *Never forget that, Rainey Bennett.*

When she felt recovered enough to meet his glance, she discovered him studying her prized serigraph of the Nantucket Lighthouse painted by Thomas McKnight. It hung next to her own paintings, the few that hadn't yet been purchased by the authors of those books.

He suddenly turned in her direction, catching her staring at him. She didn't look away, but heat scorched her cheeks.

"Would you bring your dog's picture when you come?"

She shouldn't have been surprised he'd seen the small framed photo perched on her desk. He noticed everything. What intrigued her was the reason why he'd made the request.

"All right."

Their eyes held for a brief moment. "I'll see you later."

In an economy of movement he gathered the paintings and went out the door. Unable to help herself, she watched until he and the same security man named John disappeared from view.

After shutting the door she leaned against it, wondering if she was in the middle of one of her dreams about him. But six hours later she knew everything was real when John and another security man appeared at the door. They helped her to the limousine with her bags.

Insulated by glass that allowed her to look out without being seen, she enjoyed being chauffeured to the Financial District even though it was rush hour. Once they arrived in the underground parking of the Sterling building, she was whisked by private elevator to the penthouse.

When the doors opened to Mr. Payne's office suite, Rainey couldn't control the gasp that escaped her throat. It was like walking into her own painting.

Her dark-haired hero looked up from his massive oak desk and said, "Since seeing the cover on *Manhattan Merger,* I've had the same reaction as you every time I've walked in my office."

Rainey stood there speechless.

Her gaze darted from the small framed photo perched on his desk to the painting of a ship passing a lighthouse.

"No," she whispered in disbelief.

It hung on the only wall not made of glass, just the way she'd set things up in her painting.

And then there was the dynamic billionaire himself.

Dressed in the expensive-looking blue suit he'd worn to her apartment earlier, it could have been the same suit she'd put on him in the painting. Behind him loomed the Manhattan skyline, astonishingly similar to the one she'd painted for the cover.

Still in shock, she watched as he got out of his swivel chair and brought her the small picture from his desk.

"I'm afraid to look," she confessed in a shaky voice as he closed the distance between them and handed it to her.

One glance at it and her green eyes flew to his. "This dog—the face—it looks like Winston!"

He nodded. "Meet Bruno, my trusty bullmastiff."

"I don't believe it," she murmured, starting to feel light-headed. The picture slipped to the lush carpet.

Suddenly she felt a hard-muscled arm go around her. He ushered her to the nearest leather chair.

Their faces were almost touching. She could see the

alarm in those unforgettable blue eyes, feel his breath on her cheek. "You went so pale just now. I'll get you some water."

In the next instant he'd returned and put the cup to her lips.

She drank every drop hoping he would move away from her, but to her consternation he hunkered down next to her after she'd finished.

He was too close— He smelled too good— She couldn't think, let alone breathe.

"Better now?" The concern in his deep voice was too much.

"I—I'm fine. Thank you." She stood up abruptly in an effort to separate herself from him.

The picture was still lying on the floor. Needing something physical to do in her chaotic state, she walked over and picked it up. To her relief the glass hadn't broken. At last she had the answer to why he'd requested she bring her picture of Winston along.

She put it back on his desk before turning to him. "Mr. Sterling—"

"Surely we're beyond the formalities," he broke in.

No! We aren't! We can't be!

"My name is Payne."

I know. I don't dare use it.

Her body was trembling. "I swear I've never been in your office before!"

Lines marred his rugged features. "After your testimony in court and the way you almost fainted just now, you think I don't know that?"

She put a hand to her throat. "I don't see how I could have painted everything so true to life! There's such a thing as coincidence. But *this* is something else…"

"My feelings exactly."

Rainey shook her head. "I'm not one to believe in an out-of-body experience that brought me to this office."

"Nor I."

She stared at him once more. "I'm frightened. How do you explain something like this happening?"

He rubbed the back of his neck before eyeing her through narrowed lids. "The judge said it. Some things can't be explained. You just have to accept them."

"But your fiancée probably won't believe I haven't been stalking you. *I* wouldn't!" Warmth rosied her cheeks.

His expression grew solemn. "That's why I want you with me when we tell her and Catherine the true situation."

"Your niece?"

"Yes."

"How old is she?"

"Fifteen."

"Are you two close?"

"Very," he whispered. "I shouldn't have favorites, but when you meet her, you'll understand why."

Rainey moaned. "I have to assume they've both been to your office."

He nodded. "Catherine, many times."

"When they saw the cover, they must have been petrified. I'm so sorry—" Rainey blurted.

"Don't you think you've beaten yourself enough?" There was an edge to his tone that silenced her. "Let's agree it's been a hellish week for everyone concerned and get out of here."

By now he'd reached the elevator and stood there a male entity of barely suppressed energy waiting to break free of the confining walls of his office.

Her heartbeat accelerated to a sickening pitch. Since coming to this office, being touched by him, she felt a stronger connection to him than ever.

This was wrong, all wrong. Yet she found herself taking one step, then another, toward him.

Her conscience screamed at her to beg off with some excuse before it was too late.

Still she kept going.

The doors closed, sealing her inside with him. So much for listening to the nagging voice that told her she would live to regret this.

They rode to the roof where his helicopter sat waiting.

She should stop this madness now, before things went any further. But the temptation to go where he led was greater than any force she'd ever known.

He walked to the helicopter with her and helped her get in. The security man she'd drawn in the courtroom for the judge followed them at a short distance. He climbed in behind her.

After fastening the seat strap, she realized she'd become an eager participant in a plan that could lead to her destruction. Yet one look at Payne Sterling sitting in the co-pilot's, so alive and vital, and no power on earth could tear her away.

The whir of the rotors drowned out the last death gasp of her conscience. There was liftoff.

Rainey was being carried beyond the point of no return.

CHAPTER FIVE

AFTER court, Payne had decided to spend the night at the penthouse working. In phone calls to both Catherine and Diane, he'd told them they could stop worrying. All would be explained when he arrived at Phyllis's on Friday evening.

He'd made arrangements for Diane to be picked up and driven to his sister's home where they'd have dinner. The two women had no idea he was bringing a guest.

Catherine would be delighted.

Diane would be disappointed the two of them weren't going to be alone. But her relief when she met the artist and found out Rainey was no stalker would go a long way to help make up for it.

More aware of the woman seated behind the pilot than he wanted to be, Payne let Mac do the honors of orienting her during the flight. But they were nearing Crag's Head now.

He turned his head in her direction. "We'll be putting down shortly. From there it's a short drive to my sister's house."

Rainey nodded her well-shaped head whose hair gleamed a silvery gold in the late afternoon rays of the sun. He could tell she was loving every minute of the ride. Her eyes were drinking in everything.

So were his.

He couldn't seem to get enough of her charming profile or the mold of her body in the attractive yellow sundress with the white short-sleeved jacket she was wearing.

On impulse he told his pilot to circle Crag's Head before landing. The stark whiteness of the remodeled lighthouse against the vivid blue of the ocean never failed to thrill him. He wondered what her artist's eye would make of the view.

Her reaction wasn't long in coming.

When the helicopter dipped toward his property, she cried out in awe, turning her head every which way to keep it in sight. The pilot swung around, giving her the full treatment.

"Oh—" she exclaimed again in what sounded like absolute delight. "It resembles Le Corbusier's chapel at Ronchamps I once visited. Yet it's a lighthouse too. The integration is pure genius. It's the most fabulous thing I've ever seen!"

Her shining green eyes fused with his. "Is it a museum? Can you go inside?"

Her ecstatic response pleased him in ways he didn't dare contemplate. "I think it could be arranged."

The comment produced a grin from his pilot who circled lower to land on the pad.

"You mean we're going to go inside *now?*" She sounded incredulous and so excited he could feel it in every atom of his body.

As they touched down, Payne unstrapped himself to help her out of the helicopter. When her arm brushed against his chest by accident, it felt like a lick of flame.

At the same time he breathed in the delicious scent of

spring flowers drifting around her as it had done in his office. The fragrance enticed rather than overpowered.

Sam and Andy had already pulled up in the limo to meet them. Payne cupped her elbow as he made the introductions. "I'm going to show Ms. Bennett around, then we'll leave for my sister's."

He didn't miss the speculative glance Mac gave him before the men started transferring bags and paintings from the helicopter to the limo.

Mac had every reason to look surprised. Payne guarded his privacy with a vengeance. No outsiders. Only family, Diane's family, his security people, the Myers and Drew Wallace were allowed. To the rest of the world, Crag's Head was off limits.

By bringing Rainey here, Payne had broken his own rule, another aberration that didn't bear close scrutiny.

Her gaze continued to study the exterior as they walked toward the north entrance. "This is your home," she said in a quiet voice. "The lighthouse should have been my first clue."

"Yes."

"How do you bear to leave it?"

He sucked in his breath. "I ask myself that question every morning when I climb in the helicopter."

She paused in front of the door, eyeing him with a directness he found exhilarating. "Now it's clear to me where the king of glass does his inspired thinking. Your office is simply a place where you get everyone else to carry out your business."

How did she know so much?

He cocked his head. "You read *World Fortune Magazine?*"

"No. Grace Carlow showed me the article so I'd have some idea of the man I'd be facing in court."

Her mouth suddenly curved into a haunting smile. It said she understood the forces that drove him.

The woman had second sight. Her painting was already proof of that.

"Shall we go inside?"

Her expectant expression gave her away. "I can't wait."

Payne's lips twitched before he used his pocket remote to gain entrance. Mrs. Myers met them in the foyer. She covered her surprise well at seeing him with another woman besides Diane.

"Betty? This is Rainey Bennett, an artist from Grand Junction, Colorado, now living in New York. As soon as I shower and change, we'll be driving to my niece's for dinner."

"Would you like something to drink while you wait, Ms. Bennett?"

"No thank you."

"What about you, Mr. Sterling?"

"Nothing for me either."

"If there's anything I can do, let me know."

"Thanks, Betty."

When she disappeared he turned to his guest. "While I'm upstairs, make yourself at home. I won't be long."

Fifteen minutes later he came back down knowing exactly where to find her. Sure enough she'd rolled a stool over to his underground map of Los Angeles. She was so deep in concentration she didn't hear his footsteps when he entered this portion of the house.

It took the ringing of his cell phone to bring her head

around. She got up from the stool. "How long have you been standing there?"

"A few minutes." He checked the Caller ID. It was Diane. He put the phone back in his pocket. "I do believe you find those maps as fascinating as I do."

"Fascinating isn't even the word. To tunnel under a city not knowing exactly what you'll find must provide the same kind of thrills experienced by an explorer or an astronaut."

"It's a world of rats and muck," he muttered.

"And ancient artifacts," she added. "Between you and Frontenac, the stories you could tell!"

Her reference to Bonnie Wrigley's testimony made him smile. "I have to admit it's exciting when we find something."

"Ooh I'd love to be with you the next time you come across an old burial mound."

There she went again, infecting him with her unique brand of enthusiasm. "I'll keep that in mind."

An impish smile broke out on her face. "You don't fool me. You're no ordinary engineer. It's obvious you love making sense out of a bewildering maze like this.

"When I was studying art at the university, I had to take some architecture and mechanical engineering classes as part of the curriculum. I was pulled a lot of ways back then before I ended up going for my fine arts degree.

"The fact is, I almost changed majors and went into engineering. The kind you do is probably the most challenging of all. It's another world down there under the streets. I marvel at the way you have figured it all out and then put your vision to paper.

"You see what nobody else sees and know how it's

going to work. It's miraculous. What I'd give to work alongside you and learn from you.''

Her vivacious eyes wandered over him.

"To know what can be connected to what, and make it function means you'll never run out of new challenges, you lucky man. Do you know how many people would kill to love their work the way you do?''

"You mean the same way you love yours?'' He moved closer to her, enjoying their conversation more than he'd enjoyed anything else in years.

"I enjoy what I do,'' she said. ''But I don't wake up every morning surrounded by this sea and this sky. I really can't find the words, but you already know them because you were the first one to visualize everything.

"There's so much beauty of shape and flowing line integrated with the lighthouse, it makes me want to cry.'' Tears clouded her exquisite green eyes. ''If you knew me better, you'd know I cry a lot,'' she confessed on a self-deprecating laugh. ''That's the way beauty affects me.''

Payne could relate. Right now he was looking at someone incredibly beautiful both inside and out.

"While the pilot circled your home, my mind's eye began making sketches. Now that I've been inside, it won't stop. I promise I won't put anything to paper, but if you see me experiencing symptoms of withdrawal within the next twelve hours, have some compassion.''

He burst into full-bodied laughter. Payne couldn't remember the last time that had happened. He couldn't remember ever enjoying a woman this much before. They related on a level that needed no words.

It felt good. She made him feel good. Too good.

He felt...alive.

"Mr. Sterling?"

Mrs. Myer's voice jerked him from certain private thoughts that were both exhilarating and alarming in their implication.

"Yes, Betty?"

"Your niece is on the house phone wondering where you are."

He hadn't even heard it ring. "Tell her I'll be there within ten minutes."

"Yes, sir."

"We'd better go so you don't keep them waiting any longer," Rainey murmured.

She was right.

But Payne didn't want to go.

He wanted...

No.

Don't say it, Sterling. Don't even think it.

"Are you hungry?" he asked as they started for the hallway.

"I'm getting there."

Payne had been *there* since the first moment he'd seen her in the courtroom. He recognized all the symptoms of an appetite that was growing out of control.

He should have sent Mac for the paintings, but some irresistible force had propelled him to Rainey's apartment door instead. That same force had prompted him to manufacture a reason to see her again.

And after tonight, what then?

The answer was simple. There couldn't be an after.

Tomorrow his pilot would fly her back to the city. Andy would make certain she was driven to her apartment. Payne would destroy all evidence of Ms. Bennett's brief appearance in the scheme of things.

With her gone, his newly fabricated life since the shooting would once again resume its required pattern.

But even as he rehearsed those thoughts in his mind, his hand came in contact with her silken-clad skin. Somehow her dress had ridden up while he was helping her into the back of the limo.

Both their bodies trembled from the contact before she scrambled to the other side of the limo with a speed he hadn't thought possible.

His body tautened. She was as aware of him as he was of her.

"Is your niece caught up in politics like her mother?"

The innocuous question came after they'd left the parking area on the north side of the house. With Mac and John inside the car, she couldn't have chosen a better topic.

"No. She'll be a philanthropist one day."

"Sounds like she takes after her uncle."

"Hardly. Catherine was born compassionate."

"What a rare and wonderful trait that is. I'm looking forward to meeting her."

Payne stared out the window with unseeing eyes. Like water cascading to the pool below, Catherine would gravitate to Rainey. Like Payne, she wouldn't be able to help herself.

"Tell me about your fiancée. Does she have a career?"

He'd wondered when Rainey would get around to Diane.

"Her background is English literature. Until the accident she worked for a magazine put out by Blakely College, her alma mater.''

"I'm impressed. Blakely's a prestigious women's college. I had a friend who tried to get in. She was a straight-A student with lots of other credentials going for her, but she was still turned down.''

He nodded. "It's very competitive. What happened to your friend?''

"She ended up at Vassar.''

They both started to chuckle at the same time.

This was something new for him. To be with a woman who could read his mind, who laughed and found joy over the same things. Whose thoughts were bound to his, especially during the silences.

Phyllis's house came into view.

Too soon their ride was over. Now he would have to share Rainey, then let her go. She would take all the sunshine with her.

Though she hadn't left yet, he could already feel his desolation. It shook him to the foundations.

"Uncle Payne!" His niece hurried across the back lawn with Lady at her heels. "We thought you'd never get here!"

She opened the limo door to hug him. Then her gaze caught sight of the surprise he'd brought with him.

"Catherine Boyce? Meet Rainey Bennett.''

"Hello— It's nice to meet you," his niece said with a friendly smile.

Rainey smiled back. "I've been looking forward to meeting you, Catherine. You've got an uncle who's crazy about you.''

"I love him too.''

"Sweetheart? Rainey's the artist who painted those

romance covers including *Manhattan Merger*. Since you're the one who brought that particular book to my attention, I thought you'd like to meet her. She'll be spending the night here as our guest.''

''You're kidding.'' Her light blue eyes stared at him. ''You're *not* kidding.''

Her gaze flew to Rainey's once more. ''*You* did the pictures of Uncle Payne?''

By now Mac held the door open for Rainey while the other men took the bags and paintings in the house.

His guest remained in the seat. ''Guilty as charged.''

''You're an amazing artist.''

''It's not true, but thank you.''

''Nyla's not going to believe it.''

''Who's Nyla?''

''She's been with our family for years. When she's through reading her monthly mailing of romance novels, she gives them to me. The cover on *Manhattan Merger* worried her enough to say something about it. I couldn't believe how much it looked like Uncle Payne, so I showed it to him.''

A shadow darkened Rainey's expressive features. ''I'm sorry it frightened all of you so much. You have no idea how badly I feel.''

''It's over,'' Payne declared. ''I've assured my niece there's nothing to fear. Why don't we go inside and eat dinner before it's ruined.''

Within seconds they'd alighted from the limo and the three of them started toward the back door of the house. Payne paused midstride because Lady had made Rainey's acquaintance and was now enjoying a nice scratch behind the ears.

With her tail wagging in excitement, it appeared Ms. Bennett had just acquired another admirer.

"I cooked hamburgers and potato salad for us, Uncle Payne. You should have told me you were bringing company. I would have made something special."

Rainey caught up to them. "Hamburgers have always been a favorite around my house," she spoke up. "In fact my brother still lives on them. If you tried to feed him something like chicken cordon bleu, he'd slip it to our dog."

Catherine laughed. "What kind do you have?"

"An English bulldog."

"Oh how cute. Uncle Payne once had a bullmastiff."

"I know. I saw the picture of him on his desk. The two dogs' faces look a lot alike."

"What's his name?"

"Winston."

"Of course. Winston Churchill. How funny."

"I agree." Rainey chuckled. "There are moments when my dog looks just like him. Once Craig bought a cigar and put it in Winston's mouth while I took the picture."

They both laughed.

"I'd love to see that!" his niece said.

Rainey's eyes swerved to Payne's. "I have a picture in my purse."

"Can I look?"

"Of course." Rainey opened her handbag and handed her the framed picture showing Winston with the cigar.

Catherine broke into more laughter. "This is hilarious. He's darling!"

"I think so too. He's the dog I put in the painting. Just being with Lady makes me homesick for him."

His niece darted Payne a relieved glance before handing the picture back to Rainey.

"Lady's one of the reasons I didn't go to Mexico with my family."

Payne put his arm around Catherine's shoulders. "What's the other reason?" He knew there had to be one.

"It probably has to do with a boy," Rainey inserted. "I can remember missing a few trips to hang around my brother and his friends."

Catherine smiled without saying anything. It was as good as an admission. She opened the door so they could all go inside the house.

Being an artist obviously made Rainey an excellent judge of human nature. But being around her had knocked him off base until he didn't recognize himself anymore.

He took a fortifying breath. "Where's Diane?"

"I left her on the west patio. We'll be eating out there."

"Good. Why don't you show Rainey where to freshen up while I go find her."

"I'll be happy to. Come through here, Rainey."

"Your home is fabulous, like walking into a page of *Architectural Digest*. And it's so big! My studio apartment could fit in this one room alone."

"Where do you live?"

Their voices grew faint as Payne made his way to the patio. He would love to eavesdrop on their conversation, but Diane was waiting.

"At last!" she cried when she saw him in the doorway. "I tried to reach you on the phone."

I know.

She wheeled around the table and lifted her arms to him. "It feels like two years instead of two days."

He wished to heaven he could say the same thing back to her, but he couldn't. It wasn't in him. All he could do was give her a quick kiss and hug.

As the opening line of *Manhattan Merger* had stated, Logan Townsend wasn't in love with his fiancée.

Payne wasn't in love with his fiancée either.

He'd never be able to say the words she wanted to hear.

Guilt and the need to find a cure for her had prompted his proposal of marriage. He'd told her he would take care of her and protect her. He owed her that much.

The grand plan was to help her walk again. Since their engagement he'd been working toward that goal with a single-mindedness he wouldn't allow anything to overshadow, especially not Diane's defeatist attitude.

What he hadn't counted on was Rainey Bennett entering his life.

"Are you sure everything's all right?" Diane asked when he straightened.

After pushing her wheelchair back to the table, Payne sat down next to her and reached for her hand.

"As I told you on the phone last evening, you don't need to worry anymore. To prove it, I've invited someone to dinner who will put any fears you have to rest."

Her face closed up. "You brought company here?"

"Yes. Catherine will be out with her in a minute. Her name is Lorraine Bennett. She's a freelance artist from Grand Junction, Colorado, who designs greeting cards and does paintings that appear on some of the covers for Red Rose Romance. She's the one who painted me."

"She confessed to it in court?"

"Yes. But when you hear the whole story, you'll understand it was an honest mistake."

Her eyes flashed in anger. "How could it be an honest mistake when she did it without your permission?"

"It's complicated. You'll just have to trust me."

Diane's hand clutched his. "I wish you'd asked me before you issued your invitation."

"It's because of your reaction right now that I didn't," Payne explained in a calm voice. "When the hearing started, I felt exactly like you. I was convinced someone would be arrested by the end of the day. We can thank God the reverse was true."

Her lips tightened. "For once I think you used the wrong judgment by bringing her here."

Payne happened to agree with her, but not for the same reasons she was thinking.

"I had another motive in mind, aside from the hope that meeting her would help you and Catherine to forget this incident."

"What motive?"

"Ms. Bennett feels terrible for what happened. It might help her to recover faster if she can see we bear no malice."

"She *should* feel terrible."

Payne knew it was her helplessness that made her less forgiving than she would otherwise be.

"Try to put yourself in her place, Diane. Throughout the hearing she felt the burden of being the one who not only implicated herself, but the author and the whole company."

She let go of his hand. "Why don't you find out

what's keeping them? The sooner dinner is over, the sooner she'll be gone and we can be alone. I need to talk to you about our honeymoon. I've decided where I want to go and it's not Switzerland.''

''Let's discuss this later.''

''It'll be a waste of time, Payne.''

He grimaced. ''Until we've done every earthly thing possible to help you, you don't have the right to say that. I'll be back in a minute.'' In a few swift strides he left the patio.

''Payne—''

He could hear her calling him back, but for once he refused to give in to her tears.

CHAPTER SIX

WHEN Rainey saw Payne in the kitchen doorway, his whole expression had undergone a change. He was gripped by some dark, powerful emotion held barely in check.

The difference in him was so startling, she almost dropped the plates of freshly cut fruits and vegetables she was holding.

"What's going on in here?"

Catherine must have noticed the difference in him too, but all she said was, "We're bringing the food right now, Uncle Payne. I was just introducing Rainey to Nyla. She's going to eat with us so she can hear everything that happened in court."

"Aye, aye, Captain."

Payne's comment provoked a laugh from his niece who carried the platter of hamburgers out of the kitchen. But Rainey had an idea Catherine wasn't fooled by his sudden playfulness. Neither was Rainey.

She followed them to the patio. Nyla brought up the rear with the salad she'd taken from the fridge.

If Rainey hadn't already been to Payne's home, she would have thought the Boyce's house and view of the ocean was the most beautiful sight she'd ever seen.

Everything was picture perfect against the twilight backstop.

Payne took his place behind his fiancée.

That one defining gesture set the boundaries in concrete for Rainey. What had transpired before this moment was history. Whatever happened from here on out belonged to someone else's future. Rainey was simply a spectator passing through.

"Rainey Bennett? May I present my fiancée, Diane Wylie."

"How do you do, Ms. Bennett."

The other woman spoke first and held out her hand. Rainey moved around the table to shake it.

She and Diane were probably the same age. The attractive brunette had that girl-next-door look. To Rainey's eye she seemed the type her brother might date rather than—

Rainey forced herself to stop with the speculation. Payne Sterling meant nothing to her. He couldn't!

"I'm so thankful for this opportunity to meet you, Ms. Wylie. You'll never know how sorry I am for putting all of you through more anguish."

Payne's fiancée studied Rainey out of intelligent brown eyes before letting go of her hand. "Payne said it was an honest mistake, so it's best forgotten. I'm afraid his concern over my welfare has caused him to impose on your time."

"It's not an imposition!" Rainey blurted. "We've just come from his office. I almost had a heart attack when I saw how similar everything was to my painting. Anyone would be suspicious.

"After what you've suffered, I wanted to meet you in person and assure you I meant no harm. I hope in time you can forget it."

"Rainey? Do you want to come and sit between Nyla and me?"

Rainey could have hugged Catherine for smoothing a difficult moment for her. She took her place, determined to avoid any eye contact with her host.

No more thinking about him.

"The hamburgers and potato salad are the best, sweetheart," he said after all of them had settled down to eat.

"Thanks. There's more in the kitchen."

"Everything's delicious," Rainey declared. Since meeting Diane Wylie, she'd lost her appetite but forced herself to eat in order not to hurt Catherine's feelings.

The dog brushed against Rainey's leg.

"Is it against the rules to give Lady a nibble? She's looking up at me with soulful eyes."

The teenager smiled. "You can feed her some strawberries."

"Oh good." Rainey let one drop. Lady snatched it before it reached the ground. She dropped a couple more. "Winston likes these too, but he hates grapes."

"Lady hates limes."

"I should think so." She chuckled.

"Why don't you tell us how you happened to paint my fiancé?"

Rainey had been waiting for that question. Before she could say anything, Payne rose to his feet.

"Just a minute, Rainey," he said, moving to the door. "First I want to get your brother's photograph and your artwork." Seconds later he returned and propped the fourteen-by-twenty inch paintings on some of the extra chairs.

Nyla and Catherine got up to study them. "I didn't know you did full-size paintings like these for the covers," the maid exclaimed. "They must take a long time."

"A lot of work goes into them because I do sketches first until I know exactly what I want the finished product to look like."

Nyla turned an animated face to Rainey. "It's exciting to have you here. To think you've done all those wonderful paintings. You're a fabulous artist."

"You are!" Catherine cried.

"Thank you."

"Nyla? Will you hand me the one of Payne in his office, please?"

"Here you go." The maid removed the dishes and placed the painting in front of Diane.

She examined it for a minute, then lifted her head to scrutinize Rainey. "Did you get permission to paint this woman?"

Payne's attorney was the person Rainey had expected to be adversarial, not his fiancée. But then Mr. Wallace wasn't the wheelchair-bound woman desperately in love with his client.

Rainey took a steadying breath. "Yes. She's a licensed model I've used in several covers. But sometimes I paint from memory. That's how I happened to draw Mr. Sterling."

Without preamble she spent the next ten minutes telling the same story she'd related in the courtroom. Combined with Payne's explanations regarding Bonnie Wrigley's testimony, they covered all the essentials.

Rainey let her see the photo of Winston. Between that picture, her brother's photograph and Payne's assertion that Rainey's apartment contained a serigraph of the

Nantucket Lighthouse, she hoped Catherine and Diane were satisfied.

"Because of this experience, the judge ordered that all the artists at Red Rose Romance work with licensed models from now on."

"I should think so," Diane muttered.

"I'm fairly certain they do anyway."

"Why not you?"

"Because there are times when I can't find the right model for what I want to convey. As I explained, sometimes a face in the crowd or a picture jumps out at me. I don't even know it's happening."

"You mean like my fiancé's."

"Yes," Rainey answered honestly.

Old fears had been put to rest. Now there was a new one.

The other woman believed Rainey was interested in Payne.

What better way to expose Rainey than force a confrontation which would embarrass her in front of him and his niece?

Little did Diane know she had nothing to fear from Rainey. Now was the time to prove it.

"Because I'm an artist, I can't help looking at every face a little differently than most people do. Mr. Sterling is handsome in a rugged sort of way, but so are a lot of men. Some of the male models are breathtaking."

Nyla nodded. "You can say that again!"

Bless you, Nyla.

"It's what I read in a person's face that makes it memorable. Mr. Sterling's exudes character, confidence, hard work, struggle, determination, a passion for life. All those qualities combine to make him stand out as a heroic figure, artistically speaking."

"Whoa! Uncle Payne—" Catherine smiled at him. "Did you hear all that?"

"I did," his voice grated.

Ignoring him, Rainey put Craig's photograph in front of Diane again. "Take another look at your fiancé."

Now Rainey was the one forcing his fiancée to cooperate when it was the last thing Diane wanted to do.

"See the way he's staring at the formations above the river? His eyes appear to be looking beyond them at something else the rest of us can't see. You can tell his mind is caught up in an inner vision. *That's* what makes him an arresting figure.

"That's why I suddenly found myself sketching him weeks later. He seemed perfect for certain novels I was sent. When *Manhattan Merger* came along, it was almost a spiritual mating of man and story."

The other woman's dark brows puckered. "When you're such a fine artist, why do you go to so much trouble for an inconsequential romance?"

Rainey had been waiting for a comment like that to surface. It was only natural for a woman like Diane. She'd never read a paperback romance and dismissed them as so much drivel.

"Millions of women will tell you they find them irresistible. Therefore it matters to the publishing company that their vast readership keeps coming back for more.

"Speaking from a personal note, it means everything to the author that the hero and heroine on the cover do justice to her superbly crafted relationship novel.

"That's *my* job.

"If I've done it right, the romance reader escapes even further into the story."

"I can vouch for that," Nyla piped up. "I still read the book if the cover's bad, but when it's a good one, it makes it even more exciting."

"Especially like that novel with Uncle Payne as a Viking! It was such a good story I checked out some books at the library about the Norsemen."

Rainey nodded. "It was written by a male author who's a Scandinavian history buff. I did the same thing as you, Catherine, and went to the library before I started to paint.

"You'll never know how much fun I had with that cover because the author had based Roald on a true historical figure. The clothes I put on him were the same ones on display at a museum in Norway."

"It was thrilling all right," Nyla murmured, "but I think I liked your cover of Mr. Sterling on *The Baby Doctor's Baby* the best."

"Oh, Uncle Payne—the little baby you were holding was so sweet."

"Is that right," he drawled.

Rainey forgot the promise she'd made not to look at him. Their eyes met. His were smiling. They filled her with warmth. She hurriedly glanced at Catherine.

"That was Matt, my best friend's baby boy."

"You just wanted to squeeze him," Nyla said with a sigh. "I can still see those big dimples and adorable blue eyes."

"Someday I want a baby that looks just like him."

"Let's make that about ten years away, sweetheart."

"Uncle Payne—"

Everyone laughed except his fiancée whose gaze remained leveled on Rainey.

"How did you happen to end up painting covers on romance novels of all things?"

"One day while I was in the media center of the high school where I taught art, I came across a book called *Writer's World U.S.A.* I started looking through the pages at the hundreds of publishing companies that use artwork.

"On a whim I sent out queries. Sometimes I got an answer back. Sometimes not. A few times I was asked for a sample of my work.

"To my delight, Red Rose Romance asked to see my portfolio. I sent in my disk and they hired me. I was hired by Global Greeting Cards the same way."

"You're very talented."

Diane sounded tired. Not only of the subject, but physically worn out.

"Thank you, Ms. Wylie. Once again, I'd like to apologize for the pain I unknowingly caused you. I hope you'll be able to get past this."

"I already have," she muttered. "It's obvious you meant no harm. I wish you luck in your future endeavors."

"I want the same thing for you. Have you set a date for your wedding?"

"August first."

The words cut like a knife through Rainey's heart. "That's not far away."

"You're right," Payne broke in. "Diane and I still have an important matter to decide. If you'll excuse us, we'll say goodnight." He rose to his feet.

''See you tomorrow, sweetheart. That was a terrific meal.'' He kissed Catherine's cheek.

''Goodnight, Ms. Bennett.''

''Goodnight,'' Rainey whispered.

''Nyla?'' He patted the maid's shoulder. ''Don't ever change.''

The second he wheeled his fiancée into the house, Catherine turned to Rainey. ''If I brought you some paper, would you do a picture of Lady?''

Rainey wanted to hug her for making the request. The announcement of Payne Sterling's imminent marriage had come as a greater blow than she would have imagined.

When Rainey got upset, she always turned to her drawing board for solace. Right now she was in agony.

''I'd be honored. In fact while we were eating dinner, I sketched her in my mind.''

''You mean it?'' Catherine looked stunned.

''Yes. I've already given the drawing a title.''

''What?''

Nyla looked equally curious.

She winked. ''You'll see.''

Both of them smiled.

''I'll find you some paper and a pencil!'' Catherine cried.

''There's no need for that. The art case next to my overnight bag has everything I'll require.''

''I'll get it!''

Lady raced after her.

''She's a darling girl,'' Rainey murmured as Payne's niece disappeared inside the house.

The maid nodded. ''You're coming here this evening

has made her happier than I've seen her in a long, long time.''

''Why do you say that?''

''Her younger brother, Trevor, died of leukemia last year. She took it harder than the oth—''

''Leukemia—''

''Oh…I didn't realize you didn't know. I guess I shouldn't be surprised Mr. Sterling didn't tell you. Too many similarities between the book and his life.''

''Dear God, Nyla.''

''It's been a difficult year. First his nephew's death, then Ms. Wylie's horrible accident. He's determined that she'll walk again, but she fights him so. I'm afraid Mr. Sterling has had about as muc—''

''Here you go.''

Catherine reappeared so fast, Nyla didn't get the opportunity to finish what she was going to say. Rainey was still so shaken by the news of another tragedy befalling the Sterling family, she felt ill.

Bonnie Wrigley wouldn't believe it when Rainey phoned to tell her that Payne's nephew had died from leukemia.

How many more uncanny coincidences were waiting to come to light Rainey didn't know about yet?

Nyla's revelation cast a new twist on the old adage about truth being stranger than fiction. Chills ran through Rainey's body.

With trembling hands she opened her case and removed the items she would need.

''Do you want Lady to pose for you? I can make her sit still for a few minutes.''

''Thanks, Catherine, but it won't be necessary.''

''Do you mind if I stand behind you and watch?''

"Of course not."

Lady plopped down next to them. She might not know what was happening, but she acted as if she did. The retriever had a beautiful head.

It didn't take long for the drawing to come to life. Pretty soon Nyla, who'd been taking dishes in the house, came back out to join Catherine. "Will you look at that…"

"I don't see how you do it."

"Believe me, Catherine, neither do I."

"It's a gift," Nyla stated.

"One that landed me in a lot of trouble," Rainey's voice shook.

"Uncle Payne's forgiven you. Otherwise he would never have brought you home with him."

"Well, now that I've apologized to Ms. Wylie, we need to destroy those paintings so she won't ever be reminded of them again."

"Destroyed?" they both cried at once.

"Yes. That's what the judge ordered. If you'd dispose of them, Nyla, it will save Mr. Sterling having to deal with any more grief."

"You're right. If it's a legal matter I suppose now's as good a time as any to take care of them."

"Thank you, Nyla."

While the maid picked them up and carried them into the house, Rainey finished fleshing out the drawing. In the top left-hand corner she put, "To Catherine." Down in the right-hand corner she titled it, then wrote the date and her initials.

"There." She carefully removed the sheet of paper and handed it to Catherine.

The teen held it at both ends. "The Beggar." She broke into laughter. "That's perfect! I *love* it! I'm going to have this framed and put it above my bed. Excuse me while I show it to Nyla. Then I'm going to run it upstairs so it won't get damaged."

Alone for the moment, Rainey glanced at her watch. It was quarter to eleven. They'd been out on the patio for a long time.

She got up and put everything in her case including her brother's photograph. The picture of Winston went back in her purse. On the way indoors she met Nyla.

"Where will I be sleeping tonight?"

"Up in the guest room next to Catherine's. I'll get your overnight bag and take you there."

"I'd appreciate that, but before we go, I have another favor to ask."

"What is it?"

"Could you manage to bring me a photograph of Trevor without Catherine finding out?"

The maid eyed her with a knowing expression. "You bet. There's one she carries in her wallet. It's her favorite. I'll get it."

Within fifteen minutes everyone had said goodnight. By the time Rainey had prepared for bed, Nyla returned with the photo.

Thankful for an important project that would help keep her thoughts off Payne and his fiancée, Rainey got started on the picture. Instead of using a pencil, she decided to work with her pastels. She wanted this gift to be perfect.

In the snap, Trevor appeared to be nine or ten years old and bore a strong resemblance to his sister. Several times throughout the night tears rolled down Rainey's cheeks to think he'd had to die so early in life.

At five in the morning she was finally satisfied with her work. She'd depicted him and Catherine sitting out on the back lawn. Lady lay at their feet with Catherine's arm thrown loosely around her brother's shoulders.

After putting the pastels away, Rainey climbed into bed exhausted. But two hours later and sleep still hadn't come. She'd sopped her pillow and couldn't stand to lie in bed any longer.

Meeting Payne Sterling had changed her in ways she was terrified to contemplate.

Though his fiancée might not be the warmest person, after what had happened to her, Rainey couldn't fault her for anything. She had courage to get on with her life, to marry the man of her dreams.

Why would Rainey want to torture herself by hanging around a few more hours just to be with him one more time when his devotion to Diane Wylie was unquestioned. Heavens—they would be married in another month!

If Rainey didn't take control of herself and the situation right now, then there wasn't that much difference between her and the stalker who'd put his fiancée in the wheelchair.

Calling on her inner strength, Rainey straightened the bed, got dressed and hurried downstairs with her cases. A man she hadn't seen before was sitting on a chair in the hall reading a sports magazine. He lifted his head.

"Good morning, Ms. Bennett. My name is Stan."

"Good morning."

How could Rainey have forgotten nothing went on in the Sterling's world without the presence of security?

"Is there someone on the Boyce staff who would drive me into the city? Mr. Sterling was going to have me flown back to New York later in the day, but I've just had a phone call that has forced me to change my plans. I need to leave now."

"Of course. I'll have a limo brought around back for you."

"Thank you. At some point you'll have to inform Mr. Sterling, but would you please wait a while? I happen to know he's with his fiancée and it's a Saturday morning. I'd hate for him to be disturbed over a matter as trivial as my transportation. She appeared very tired last night."

The security man hesitated briefly, then nodded. While he got on his radio phone, Rainey walked through the house to the back hall and let herself outside.

To her surprise there was a strong wind coming off the ocean. It filled the air with salt spray. Judging by the overcast sky, the sun might not make an appearance at all.

She would love to be at Crag's Head enjoying the elements right now. But that magnificent place and the man who lived there were forbidden to her.

You need to remove yourself from temptation and fly far away, Rainey. Much farther than your studio apartment.

By the time the limo had rolled around, she'd made up her mind to move back to Grand Junction. Coming to New York had been the biggest mistake of her life.

CHAPTER SEVEN

PAYNE walked in the back door of his sister's house at five after eight, ready for a morning swim in the ocean with Catherine and Rainey.

To his surprise Lady didn't come flying down the rear entrance hall to greet him. With a guest as exciting as Rainey to talk to, his niece had probably stayed up late last night and was sleeping in.

Rainey might still be in bed too, but Payne had a hunch she was an early riser. Somewhere in the house he imagined her hard at work on her latest art project.

In the hope she might be out on the patio where they'd had dinner, he headed in that direction. When he discovered everything was locked up tight and she was nowhere in sight, a keen sense of disappointment swept through him.

Maybe she was in the kitchen eating breakfast with the staff. But he quashed that thought the moment he spied Stan, one of his sister's security people, drinking a cup of coffee by himself.

When the other man saw him, he put down his mug. "I was going to call you in a little while."

Stan didn't have to say another word for Payne to know something had gone on he wasn't going to be happy about. Like the fact that Rainey was no longer on the premises.

"When did Ms. Bennett leave?"

"About an hour ago. Jed drove her back to the city. She asked me not to bother you since she knew you and Ms. Wylie were together."

"You're supposed to bother me. That's part of your job!" Payne bit out in a rare show of anger because Rainey's charm was so potent, she'd managed to con even a pro like Stan.

Payne shouldn't have cared. It shouldn't have mattered she'd slipped away without his knowing about it. But it did matter. Even more than he'd imag—

"Uncle Payne?"

At the sound of his niece's subdued voice he wheeled around. Both she and Nyla were standing in the doorway with Lady.

"I'm afraid it's my fault Ms. Bennett left in such a hurry this morning," Nyla murmured.

"Come and look," Catherine urged him.

On leaden feet, Payne followed them into the main dining room where he glimpsed a sheet of art paper laid out on the table.

Nyla stood at his other side. "Last night I happened to say something to Ms. Bennett about Trevor's illness because I thought she'd already been told about it. You know, after reading about the hero who had leukemia.

"I never saw anyone look as devastated as she did when she found out. Before she went to bed she asked me to bring her a photograph of him. *This* is the result."

Catherine put a hand on his arm. "I found it in the guest bedroom this morning."

He walked over to see Rainey's handiwork.

One look at the picture done in pastels and his throat almost closed from too much emotion. She'd caught it all. The love, the sweet, tender bond between brother and sister.

"It's so beautiful it hurts," Catherine whispered.

It *was* beautiful. It *did* hurt because everything Rainey drew or painted was driven by heartfelt emotions.

In the next instant his niece was sobbing quietly against Payne's shoulder. "How did she know Trev and I used to spend time out in back with Lady?"

"I guess that's part of her great talent." There didn't seem to be any other explanation.

Nyla's eyes went suspiciously bright. "She felt so badly for upsetting your family, it's evident she wanted to leave all of you with a gift that would bring you happiness. What a wonderful person she is. I've never met anyone like her."

Neither have I.

"She did another picture for me, Uncle Payne. I'll get it."

As he watched Catherine hurry from the room Nyla said, "I don't blame Ms. Bennett for setting off early. I'm sure she's anxious to forget this whole unpleasant business and move on."

Payne couldn't argue with that. After putting Rainey through the hell of a courtroom hearing, he'd forced her to face Diane who did nothing but patronize her all evening. Furthermore he'd had no right to bite Stan's head off because Rainey had reached the point where she couldn't take any more.

"You're going to love this one too." Catherine entered the dining room with another sketch in hand. He took it from her.

"'The Beggar,'" he read the words aloud. Incredibly,

Rainey had caught the special pleading expression in Lady's eyes while she waited with exaggerated patience and politeness for something to eat.

"She's left you some real treasures," Payne murmured. He put the sketch on the table next to the other picture and looked around. "Where are the paintings?"

"Rainey asked me to dispose of them."

He shot Nyla a piercing gaze. "She *what?*"

"Don't worry. I couldn't bring myself to do it. They're in my room."

"I can always count on you. Hold on to them for me. I'll get them later."

"You bet."

Adrenaline surged through his veins. If he didn't expend his excess energy soon, he'd explode.

"Catherine? Put your suit on and we'll take a swim."

"I'm already wearing it under my clothes."

"Then let's go."

"I'll have breakfast waiting for you when you get back."

"Nothing for me, Nyla," he said, "but thanks for the offer."

Forty-five minutes later he and Catherine came out of the ocean and took turns throwing a stick for Lady to fetch. Unfortunately Payne's swim had done nothing to improve his mood which was as stormy as the elements.

His niece appeared to be deep in her own thoughts. There was little conversation until they started back to the house.

"I didn't know the hero in *Manhattan Merger* almost died of leukemia, or that the author lost a child to it. Have you still got the book?"

"Yes."

"I want to read it."

"You're sure?"

"More than ever. I don't see how Diane can say that romances don't reflect real life."

"She would change her tune if she read one." Reading Ms. Wrigley's novel had been a revelation to him.

"But that's the problem. I don't think she ever will."

"Then it's her loss."

Somehow he had to find a way to break through Diane's defenses so she'd go to Switzerland. He couldn't think beyond it.

"Are you going to spend the day with her?"

"No. I have work at the office. She and her mother are overseeing the bridesmaids' fittings. What are your plans?"

"Linda and I are going to play tennis with a bunch of friends. Later I think we'll see a movie."

"Sounds fun. Be sure and take your cell phone with you so we can keep in touch."

"I will." She looked up at him. "Uncle Payne?" By now they'd reached the back lawn.

He sensed her hesitancy. "What is it?"

"When mom and dad get back, I'd like to invite Rainey over for dinner so the whole family can meet her. Would that be okay with you?"

His heart pounded like a sledgehammer. "Of course. Why do you ask?"

"Diane doesn't like me, and I could tell she really didn't like Rainey."

Tell me something I don't already know.

"Don't worry about it."

"After you're married, I hope you'll still come over a lot."

"No one will ever keep me away from you, sweet-heart."

Payne gave his niece a hug before climbing into the limo. Mac followed and shut the door.

"Take us home, Andy."

On the short drive to Crag's Head, Payne phoned his pilot and told him to get the chopper ready. He'd be taking off for the city within twenty minutes.

During his talk with Catherine on the way back from the beach, a strange feeling had come over him. Something he couldn't explain. But it all had to do with Rainey and her precipitous departure from the Sterling compound. Suddenly he felt it imperative to catch up with her.

It was close to noon when he alighted from the limo and entered her apartment building. He pressed the button and waited for a response. If she wasn't home, he'd wait outside in the limo as long as it took until she showed up.

He was ready to buzz her again when he heard static and then a man's voice said, "Yes?"

Payne froze in place. "Is this Lorraine's Bennett's studio?"

"Yes."

He struggled to keep from erupting. "May I speak to her?"

"Who is this?"

The urge to knock the man to kingdom come was growing stronger by the second.

"If she doesn't answer within five seconds, I'm coming up to find out why," Payne thundered.

"I'm here, Mr. Sterling," Rainey answered sounding out of breath.

His brows furrowed. What in the hell was she doing with a man in her apartment this early in the day unless... The pictures that ran through his mind filled him with feelings too primitive to describe.

"We have to talk. How soon will you be free?"

"I thought you and your fiancée were—never mind, it doesn't matter. Just a minute, please."

Apparently she'd left his sister's house to rejoin her lover. Out of all the reasons he'd imagined for her disappearance without telling him, Payne would never have thought it was because of a man.

But then he remembered that she'd had other plans the night before and had canceled them in order to accompany Payne. How long had this relationship been going on?

"It's all right. You can come up now."

The minute he heard the click of the door, he opened it and took the stairs three at a time to her floor. He found her standing outside her apartment with the door closed trying to appear at ease, and failing.

She also looked so damn fresh and innocent in a white cotton top and tan jeans, he found her utterly desirable. His heart slammed into his ribs.

"Aren't you going to introduce me to your friend?"

"He went back to his apartment."

How convenient.

"If this was a bad time, why didn't you just say so? I'd have come by later."

"You're a busy man, Mr. Sterling. Since you took the

time to drive over here, I didn't want you to be put out by having to come back again.''

She was hiding something from him.

''It would have been nice if you'd tried to be this thoughtful by staying put at my sister's house until you were flown home.''

She didn't move a muscle, but she couldn't prevent the blush that swept up her neck into her beautiful face.

''I was brought up to believe a good stay is a short stay. Last evening I did all I could to make your fiancée and niece feel better about what happened. When I woke up this morning, I could see no reason to prolong my visit.''

''*I* can give you one.''

Her hands rubbed the sides of her hips in a gesture she probably wasn't aware of. She didn't look quite so sure of herself now. ''I-is something else wrong?''

''I'm afraid the hallway of a busy apartment building is hardly the place to carry on the conversation I have in mind.''

Color stained her cheeks again.

''Would you prefer to come downstairs and sit in the limo while we talk?''

''No—'' she cried softly, putting a nervous hand to her throat.

''I can go to my office and come back later in the day if that would suit you better.''

''Please don't do that.'' She sounded panicked.

''Then what *do* you propose? If you were planning to spend the day with the man upstairs, just say so. We can talk tomorrow.''

''No,'' she whispered. ''You can come in for a minute.''

For a minute?

She darted inside and left the door open for him.

After crossing over her threshold, it took all his strength not to slam the door as he shut it. When he turned around, one look at her denuded walls and desk, and his body went cold.

"It looks like you're in the process of vacating the premises," his voice grated.

"Yes." There were several boxes on her couch already packed. She hurriedly moved them to the floor. "There. Now you can sit down."

He stayed where he was. "Are you moving in with him?"

She bit the soft underside of her lip in a betraying gesture that beguiled him.

"I don't mean to be rude, but I hardly believe that's anyone's concern except mine."

"It'll be my niece's when she tries to invite you to a family party once her parents get home on Monday and you can't be located."

Her gilt-blond head reared. Her eyes had gone that smoky green color again and looked haunted. "You mustn't let her do that!"

His breath caught. "After giving her back a sense of her brother with that magnificent picture she'll treasure all her life, do you honestly think she won't do whatever she can to thank you?"

"I'm glad if she liked it, but—"

"But what?" he demanded.

"I won't be here next week."

Good Lord. He knew what was coming before she said it.

"I—I'm flying home to Grand Junction tomorrow."

Payne felt as if a stalker's bullet had just pierced his heart. "You were going to leave without saying good-bye?"

"We said it last night."

"I distinctly heard you tell me goodnight," he reminded her.

She averted her eyes. "I know you think I'm running away to lick my wounds because of what happened at the hearing, but you'd be wrong," her voice trembled. "The hearing actually did me a favor because it brought my brother to New York."

The faster she talked, the more she revealed her nervousness.

"We haven't spent time together like we used to. While he was here, we talked all night. After next week Craig won't be running any more float trips. He's getting ready to open his own sporting goods company. It's been his lifelong dream.

"The bank gave him the loan and he's found space in a good location. Though he's got help, he could use a lot more."

Payne's hands formed into fists. "So you've suddenly decided to do the honors."

"I have some savings," she went on explaining, "and don't need to accept any more work for a while. I want to help him get set up."

"You're an artist! A fabulous artist. You moved to New York to follow your own dream."

"I never planned to live here forever. This was an experiment. An adventure. Nothing more."

"Does your brother know what you're about to sacrifice for him?"

"N-not yet. I'm planning to surprise him."

"I don't believe you."

"What do you mean?" She sounded angry, but anger masked fear.

"You're not running to him as much as running from something. Admit it!"

By now she was standing at the window looking out, ostensibly so she wouldn't have to face him.

"Please go, Mr. Sterling. When you see your niece, tell her goodbye for me, and let her know I'm happy she liked the picture."

"She loves both of them. The whole family will be delighted when they lay eyes on 'The Beggar.' Creating those masterpieces must have kept you up all night."

Payne hadn't been able to sleep either.

Still she said nothing.

He shifted his weight. "I'm not leaving this apartment until I learn why you planned to disappear without a trace."

Time lapsed before she said in a low voice, "You're going to make me say it aren't you."

Another surge of adrenaline electrified his body. "Say what?" he prodded.

Rainey turned her head in his direction wearing a solemn expression. "Your fiancée knows you've been to my apartment," she began in a throbbing voice.

"She knows I've been to your office, that I've ridden in your helicopter. She knows I've been out to Crag's Head. After last night she knows I was an overnight guest in your sister's home.

"If I were your fiancée, I could handle all of it knowing everything was the result of the hearing. But any more contact, even a whisper of it, and I would feel…threatened.''

He took a step closer. ''If you think moving back to Colorado removes that threat, then you're very much mistaken. You could go to the ends of the earth and it wouldn't make any difference.''

''Then you haven't done enough to make her feel secure in your love,'' she fired back.

Unable to respond to that remark without incriminating himself he said, ''She'll never feel secure about anything until she can walk again. There's a clinic in Switzerland that might be able to help her, but she refuses to let me take her.''

Upon that remark Rainey rested her body against the edge of the desk. Her head was lowered.

''I can understand why. It would be so hard to go there on a thread of hope and then find out not even those doctors could help.''

''Diane still has some feeling in her legs, Rainey. There's a chance she could walk again. Otherwise the doctors wouldn't keep urging her to go for a consultation and exam.''

Taking a calculated risk he said, ''This morning while Catherine and I were swimming in the ocean, an idea came to me that could change Diane's mind. You corroborated it moments ago when you talked about her feeling threatened.''

That brought Rainey's head up. He had her full attention now.

''Instead of putting your career on hold for your brother who still has no idea what you're planning, how would you like to do something that could result in Diane throwing away that damn wheelchair?''

A stunned expression broke out on her face. "If I thought I could help, naturally I'd do it, but I can't imagine what it would be."

Rainey Bennett—I'm going to hold you to that.

"Last evening you told me you'd give anything to work alongside me."

She shook her head. "I was carried away. You know that."

"You meant it, Rainey. So I'm proposing that you move into my home at Crag's Head and expand your artistic talents by making my maps for me. It'll be a merger financially beneficial for both of us."

An explosion of green sparks lit up her heavily lashed eyes.

"Until you came along, I never trusted anyone else to do them. With your help I'll be free to travel without the worry that I'm getting behind on the technical end. In this business I have to set up new markets before the competition does.

"In return, let's pray Diane is so threatened by your presence in my life, she'll agree to go to Switzerland and learn to walk again if only to be able to face you on an equal footing."

"You can't be serious!" She sounded aghast.

"I never say what I don't mean. You have to understand something about my fiancée. No one has more pride than Ms. Diane Wylie of the North Shore.

"Her condition is so shocking to her, it's come between her and her friends, her work on the magazine. She helped on my sister's last senatorial campaign. Once upon a time she had aspirations to go into politics herself. All that drive has vanished. She's not the same person she used to be.''

Rainey's eyes shimmered with unshed tears. "That's so tragic."

"It is," Payne murmured. "No human being deserves to suffer like she has.

"Last night I felt her pain because she used to be vital and vivacious like you, with a hell of a lot to contribute. If I thought she could be that way again, I'd move heaven and earth to make it happen."

"I'm sure you would," she whispered.

"Since Trevor's death, Catherine's been working on Diane. In her own sweet way she's tried to remind her that there never was any hope for her brother, but there is for Diane. Still my fiancée hasn't responded.

"The first signs of fight I've seen in her were last night while you were enchanting everyone." Enchanting me. "Catherine was a different girl because of you, and Diane knew it.

"With your cooperation, maybe Diane will get so angry she'll end up begging me take her to Switzerland. She's a competitor at heart. That's why I believe this will work. I could have roamed the earth and never found a more worthy opponent than you."

After a significant pause he said, "If your answer is no, then I'll leave here and you'll never have to worry about dealing with me again. If it's yes, you'll have the satisfaction of knowing you tried to help another human being get back her life."

Rainey couldn't have looked more dazed.

"I realize it's a lot to ask. I have no right. I do a lot of things when I don't have the right, but it's the way I'm made."

The silence lengthened.

Summoning every vestige of willpower he possessed, Payne walked out of the apartment with a vision indelibly impressed of her standing there looking tormented.

But not tormented enough to call him back.

With that crushing realization, he headed for the staircase.

The thought of life without Rainey Bennett sent him into a despair so black, he didn't remember going down the three flights of stairs to the foyer. Mac and John stood somewhere in the periphery waiting for Payne to climb in the back of the limo. Doors opened and closed. It was all a blur.

"Payne?"

"What is it, Andy?"

"Ms. Bennett is on the sidewalk motioning for you to put down your window."

Being told that Rainey had followed him all the way to the street was like his body freefalling thousands of feet only to be yanked as his chute suddenly opened.

With lightning speed he levered himself from the car, still trying to catch his breath.

Dozens of people were walking back and forth, but as far as Payne was concerned, he and Rainey were the only two people in existence. She couldn't very well avoid his gaze though she was trying.

"You wouldn't be standing here if the answer weren't yes. Shall we talk about it in the limo, or upstairs?"

She moistened her lips nervously. "When would you want me to start?"

"Now."

"So soo—"

"I have to leave for Paris on Tuesday morning. Therefore I'd like to go over my maps with you this weekend and show you how I work."

"But my apartmen—"

"I'll help you bring down the things you'll need for the weekend. On Monday we'll arrange for you to meet with movers. You can put anything in storage you won't require while you're living with me."

"I'll have to be here for the courier to pick up my latest painting."

"We'll do that and I'll take care of your lease."

"No—I've already made an installment agreement with the super."

Payne decided to let her have that victory for now. Early on he'd learned that when he was on the brink of a major takeover, he pounced when the tiny window of opportunity presented itself. The little things could slide.

"I—I won't need your help with my bags. If you'll wait here, I'll be back down as soon as I can."

"Take all the time you want." I'm not going anywhere without you.

Payne recognized she craved privacy to say goodbye to the man who'd been in her apartment earlier. Little did the poor devil know Rainey would be out of permanent circulation the moment of liftoff.

While he waited, he phoned his niece.

"Hi, Uncle Payne!"

"How are things?"

"Great!"

That was the most enthusiasm he'd heard out of her in a long time.

"I invited my friends over to see Rainey's drawings. Now they want her to do pictures of them and their pets so they can give them to their parents for Christmas presents. Do you think she would do it if they paid her?''

He smiled. ''Knowing Rainey, she wouldn't take the money.''

''I'm sure you're right, but that's a lot to ask when she has two other jobs.''

''Tell you what. You can ask her yourself tomorrow.''

''Did you invite her out to the house again?''

''No. I asked her to accept a full-time job with me. She said yes, and she'll be moving into Crag's Head where she'll work on my maps.''

There was a prolonged silence.

''Uncle Payne...does Diane know?''

''Not yet. I'll tell her tonight.''

''That's going to hurt her a lot.''

''I'm hoping it'll make her angry.''

He could hear her brain working. ''You *want* her to be jealous.''

''I want her to walk again. Maybe if she gets angry enough, she'll do something about it and consider going to that clinic in Switzerland.''

Another pause. ''Does Rainey know why you've asked her to come to work for you?''

''Yes. She wants to help Diane too.''

''So do I.''

''You already have. You're a sweetheart. I'm sure Rainey will enjoy your company, especially when I'm out of town. You can show her around, make certain she knows where to swim safely.''

''Do you think she likes to sail?''

''I guess we're going to find out. Come on over in the morning and have breakfast with us.''

"Will Diane be there?"

"I'll invite her. Let's hope she won't be able to stay away. Have fun this afternoon. I'll see you in the morning."

After ending the call, he made one more to his pilot to alert him they'd be flying back to Crag's Head soon.

Two hours later he experienced the sensation of déjà vu when his housekeeper met him and Rainey in the foyer.

"Mrs. Myers? Ms. Bennett has agreed to come to work for me. For the time being she'll be living here. Let's put her in the bedroom with the view of Phantom Point."

Rainey's mouth curved upward. "That sounds intriguing."

"It is. Sometimes you see it, sometimes you don't. Shall I take up your bags now, Ms. Bennett?"

"Please call me Rainey. I'll carry them."

"You're going to find out my new assistant has an independent streak," Payne murmured.

"That's fine with me as long as you call me Betty."

His housekeeper liked to keep things formal. For her to make a concession like that meant Rainey had already won her over.

"It's a deal."

"We're going to get busy in my study, Betty. When you have a moment, will you bring us some lunch?"

"Coming right up."

Payne was eager to sit down with Rainey and explain how he put his crude drawings together into one blueprint. With her intuitive eye, she would bring her own expertise to streamline the process and make innovations.

After a moment's consideration he pulled out a tube housing the drawings of Paris he'd already begun work on. While he was laying them out on the large worktable, his cell phone rang. A check of the Caller ID confirmed it was Diane.

His eyes flicked to Rainey. "I have to take this call. Go ahead and see what you make of everything."

It was like a giant jigsaw puzzle. He couldn't help but be curious how long it would take her to fit each piece together.

Moving a few feet away he answered the phone. Now that he had Rainey firmly entrenched beneath his roof, it was time to follow through with the rest of his plan.

CHAPTER EIGHT

RAINEY slept, but it was fitful. At dawn she stole from the queen-size bed to half lie in the window seat and contemplate the vast Atlantic from her bedroom high above the water. As morning broke to the sounds of gulls, she remembered something Craig had said in an attempt to comfort her.

Treat the whole experience with Payne Sterling as part of your adventure in the Big Apple.

He didn't know it then, but her brother had dispensed the best advice he could have given her. That was exactly the way she was going to look at her situation from here on out.

A marvelous adventure. The kind she enjoyed living with the heroine inside a romance novel until the very last page when she closed the book.

There *would* come a last page with Payne. Until then, what were the odds of meeting an exciting, brilliant New York billionaire-soon-to-be-trillionaire in her lifetime? Of working temporarily as his live-in assistant in his hideaway which was an architectural treasure?

Maybe a gazillion-to-one?

She leaned out the window to inhale the tangy sea air and enjoy the ocean breeze. The humidity curled the ends of her hair. Her skin, so used to the dry climate of the Colorado Rockies, felt soft and smooth.

By some quirk of fate, she and Payne had been

brought together at this moment in time. It wouldn't last, so why go on torturing herself about it?

Why not be the catalyst that might rouse his fiancée from debilitating fear so she could walk down the aisle to the man waiting for her at the altar?

What were the odds of Rainey ever playing a major role in someone else's rescue again?

The answer was, never.

"Good morning, Ms. Bennett!"

Rainey looked down to see her host walking up the beach in cutoffs and a T-shirt looking like a contemporary Jane Austen hero.

"Why if it isn't Mr. Darcy!"

His hands went to his hips. The next thing she knew he was laughing up at her. She found herself laughing with him.

Careful, Rainey. Don't let him guess the very sight of him turns your bones to liquid. Keep things light.

"If it was your intention to go about startling all the young ladies, you can consider you've accomplished your objective, sir."

"My Dear *Miss* Bennett—if I startled you, it was because you were hoping I would happen to come along at this precise moment to catch you in, shall we say, flagrante delicto? so you could be pretend to be startled."

"Oh my, Mr. Darcy. Rumors of your monumental ego combined with your insufferable arrogance have been greatly understated. Isn't it a good thing you're in love with yourself since it's probable no one else would ever be able to love you quite so well."

More laughter rumbled out of him, the deep, rich male kind.

Suddenly Rainey heard clapping. "Well done, you two. Jane Austen is alive and doing just fine at Crag's Head."

Rainey looked to the right and caught sight of Diane. "She wrote one of the great romances, don't you think, Ms. Wylie?"

"She wrote several. I found *Persuasion* her most compelling."

The mention of that particular title sounded cryptic and introduced a different mood into the tenor of the morning. Rainey could tell Payne was equally affected.

Persuasion was what was needed to get her to that clinic.

"I understand we were all going to have breakfast when you arrived. Excuse me and I'll be right down." She tore herself from the window, unwilling to put herself through the agony of watching him greet his fiancée.

Yesterday he'd worked with Rainey all afternoon and into the early evening. The rapport between them had been uncanny. She couldn't believe how well things had gone, what a remarkable teacher he was.

Being with him, she'd been unaware of time passing. It had almost killed her when seven-thirty rolled around and he'd excused himself to go pick up Diane for dinner. At some point in the evening Rainey knew he would inform his fiancée he'd hired Rainey to come to work for him.

Since Rainey hadn't seen him until he'd been walking along the surf moments ago, it was anyone's guess how Diane had reacted to his news.

Judging by her unexpected appearance on the path just

now, his plan seemed to be working to some degree. She'd plunged right into the thick of things, staking her claim in front of Rainey.

His fiancée had a lot of demons to fight besides her fear that another woman was interested in her fiancé. The last thing Rainey wanted to do was hurt her. All she could do was follow Payne's lead and hope it caused the kind of reaction that would force Diane to get past her psychological block.

Rainey pulled clothes from the closet and drawers. The temperature had dropped to the low seventies prompting her to dress in a pair of white pleated trousers and a yellow cotton pullover.

With a good brushing of her hair and an application of coral lipstick, there was nothing more to do but join them. She left the bedroom not knowing quite what to expect, but realizing that Diane was waiting for her.

The dining room off the study had its own glorious view of the ocean. Payne and Diane had already started to eat.

His gaze flicked to Rainey's. So much vital masculinity for breakfast made her heart race. "Help yourself to anything you want at the buffet."

"Thank you."

It looked like the housekeeper had outdone herself. Rainey poured herself some orange juice, then went for the sausage and eggs, her favorite breakfast.

"Come and sit down."

Said the spider to the fly?

The other woman's smile was benign enough. Yet Rainey did her bidding with a prickling awareness that

Diane had been geared for a confrontation since Payne had dropped his bombshell.

"How did you sleep, Ms. Bennett?"

Payne covered Diane's hand. "Since we're all going to be seeing a lot of each other from now on, let's get on a first name basis."

Fearing she might choke on her juice, Rainey put the glass back down. "To be honest, I was so excited to be right here on the water, I stayed awake most of the night. It's quite heavenly."

"No other woman apart from Mrs. Myers has ever slept at Crag's Head before."

His fiancée had just fired her first salvo.

"It must be thrilling for you to know that after August first this will be your home, Diane. The design transports you to another realm, yet you're firmly planted on a headland with a whole ocean at your feet. I think you're the luckiest woman alive to have all this to look forward to."

"When Payne installs an elevator, it will be more livable for me."

"If we leave for Switzerland right away, it's possible you'll never have to use another elevator again."

"It's not going to happen, Payne. But since you brought the subject up, now would be the time to say what's on my mind."

Diane's gaze swerved to Rainey who wondered what was coming next. She stopped chewing.

"I know why he hired you."

Her bold declaration revealed the fire Payne had been referring to when he'd asked Rainey to be his accomplice.

"The problem is, I'm not sure he told *you* why."

Rainey had no choice but to play dumb. "I don't think I understand."

"Those maps of Payne's are sacrosanct. No one in the hierarchy of his company is allowed inside Crag's Head to see them. He trusts no one to touch them. They're his brainchild, the key to his success.

"Then suddenly he decides to let a portrait artist who paints covers for Red Rose Romance move into his fortress and assist him on drawings that are so complicated no one but Payne himself can understand them?" She left out a brittle laugh.

"I don't think so. I may not be able to walk, but credit me with more brains than that, Rainey. We both know he's installed you here to force my hand because he wants me to go to Switzerland for an operation."

The strength it took to hold the other woman's gaze without flinching called on every nerve and muscle in Rainey's body.

"I've told him I'm not going. Of course he doesn't understand the meaning of the word no. What he's done is pull one of his shrewd business ploys to get me to capitulate by bringing a beautiful woman into his home on the pretext of working for him.

"He knows this will cause our families and friends to talk. What better way to get me to change my mind than threaten to humiliate me."

Rainey's heart sank like a stone. Though Diane's delivery had been unemotional, she had to be dying inside.

"What he refuses to accept is that there's no miracle cure waiting for me at the end of the road. I guess what I'm saying is, the next move is up to you."

She paused to take a drink of her coffee. When she put the cup down again she said, "If you truly thought he was offering you a legitimate job, and yet you continue to stay under his roof knowing what I've just told you, then it will be clear to everyone who loves him that you two are having an affair.''

A groan almost made it past Rainey's lips.

Diane had just called her fiancé's bluff. The fear that an operation wouldn't change anything was keeping her locked in that wheelchair. Rainey could weep for both of them because that fear was holding him prisoner too.

Somehow Rainey needed to say something in a counter move that would still be the truth, yet not jeopardize an already precarious situation.

''I'm aware of his hopes for you,'' she began quietly. ''It's only natural when he loves you so much, but I'm afraid the blame for the job offer lies with me.''

One of Diane's brows lifted in a patronizing gesture. ''Your attraction to him has made you the proverbial putty in his hands.''

''I *am* attracted to him,'' Rainey came back, fighting fire with fire. ''If you're talking physical attraction, then I'd be a liar if I didn't admit it considering I've done eight paintings of him already. He's an incredibly good-looking man.''

The mockery in Diane's smile started to vanish.

''If you're talking mental attraction, I admit to that too. Let me tell you why.'' Now that Rainey was all wound up, it would be therapeutic to get certain things said.

''You don't know very much about me. How could you? I grew up in a small town. My brother loves it there. From an early age on, he knew he wanted to live there forever and run a sportings goods store. Come fall, that dream is finally going to happen for him.

"I was different. I had this dream to move to a big city and see what it was like.

"The money from teaching art in public school was a means of keeping me alive, but it was my freelance jobs that paid me enough to get here. In all honesty, I came to New York hoping I might stumble on to my life. Do you know what I'm talking about?"

Diane brushed some hair away from her forehead. "People like you flock to New York every day looking for the same thing. The difference is, none of them ended up in a courtroom with my fiancé."

A tremor rocked Rainey's body.

"That's true. When the judge was reprimanding me, he said it best. *Call it destiny or fate, you happened to paint the one man whose phenomenal success in life has made him vulnerable to the ugliest elements in our society.*

"It seems that fate, or destiny, whatever you choose to call it, brought me to this house. While your fiancé was upstairs getting changed before taking me to the Boyce's to meet you, I wandered into his study. That's when something amazing happened.

"I saw his maps spread over the walls of the lighthouse. They were so fantastic, I was spellbound. I remember feeling the same way when I was young and came across Tolkien's map of Middle Earth for the first time.

"When Mr. Sterling came back downstairs ready to leave, he found me babbling with so much excitement, I'm sure he didn't know what to make of it. I practically begged for a chance to work with him."

Diane's brown eyes flared in surprise. Rainey could

be thankful for that much reaction. At least she was listening.

"Yes, I'm guilty of wanting to grab at an opportunity to work with someone like him because fate would never allow it to happen a second time. But if you're talking emotional attraction, that's something else again because he's spoken for. He's asked *you* to marry him.

"If you'd seen your fiancé in court, then you'd know he was only there for one reason. To protect *you*. To make certain nothing would ever hurt you again.

"He was a frightening adversary when he thought I'd been out there stalking the two of you. After court ended I thought how blessed you were to have a fiancé who showed that kind of devotion to you. One who'd do anything for you. He'd give his life to see you walk again!" Rainey's voice throbbed.

Diane unexpectedly averted her eyes.

"I discovered the strength of his devotion when he asked me to meet you and help reassure you that I posed no threat to your safety.

"He's a hero in every sense of the word, Diane. *Your* hero. The kind you could read about in those little romance novels whose covers I paint."

She had one more thing to say. This time she turned to Payne who'd been staring at her through shuttered eyes.

He'd enlisted her help. She'd complied with his request and would carry out her part of the bargain for a while longer. But she had to draw the line somewhere because her very existence depended on it.

"Did you tell Diane I'm only here in New York until my brother sends for me?"

"Uncle Payne?"

"In the dining room, sweetheart," he answered his niece without acknowledging Rainey's question.

"I brought Linda with me. She wants to meet Rainey."

"Hi, Linda," he drawled. "Come and have some breakfast with us."

"Thanks, Mr. Sterling."

Seconds later the two teens breezed in the room wearing shorts and tops. Linda was a tall girl with pretty features and a chestnut braid hanging down the middle of her back.

She walked over to Diane. "Hi, Ms. Wylie! How are you?"

"I'm fine, thank you." But Diane didn't sound fine at all. Her voice held a definite tremor.

"I bet you're getting excited for the wedding."

"Yes," she murmured.

"Rainey?" Catherine headed for her. "I'd like you to meet my best friend, Linda Miles. Linda? This is Rainey Bennett."

"Hello, Linda." The teen moved closer. "What beautiful hair you have."

She and Catherine exchanged smiles. "Thanks. I saw the pictures you did for Catherine. They're so good."

"What she's trying to say is, do you think you could draw one of Linda sometime?"

"I wouldn't expect you to do it for free, that is if you had the time to do it."

"I'll make the time, and I wouldn't take your money," Rainey assured her.

Their host got up to pour himself a cup of coffee. "Why don't you girls grab a plate of food?"

"Thanks. We're starving. Oh—before I forget—where did you put *Manhattan Merger,* Uncle Payne?"

"It's in my study. Left-hand drawer of my desk."

"Can I get it now so I won't forget?"

"Go ahead."

"Do you like romances, Linda?" Diane inquired as Catherine left the dining room.

After their previous conversation, Rainey had to give the other woman credit for hanging in there. Payne had said his fiancée was a competitor at heart. Rainey believed him.

"I love them," Linda said. "They're really fun."

"How do you mean fun?"

Catherine's friend found the food she wanted and sat down. "It's fun to see how two completely different people get together, the problems they have to overcome."

"Don't you know that's one of the big concerns about romances? Our magazine did an in-depth article on them some time ago. It wouldn't hurt you to read it. Those stories only show the exciting parts of a relationship, and never deal with the ever after."

"At least the couples in the romances I've read get married, Ms. Wylie. In real life a lot of them live together first, and statistics show that more of them break up later and then kill each other or something."

"Does your mother approve?"

"She doesn't mind. Mom's sick of all the violence and sex on TV."

"Don't tell me there isn't a lot of that in those books."

"Some are graphic, some aren't. What I like is that the two people are really in love and faithful to each other. There isn't any violence in them. My grandma says every man should read one so he'd know how to treat a woman better.''

Rainey drained the rest of her juice so she wouldn't smile.

"Your grandmother reads them?'' Diane sounded incredulous.

"Yes. When I had my tonsils out last year she came over and read one to me. That got me started.''

Their host chuckled. ''You're never going to win this argument, Diane.''

"Let me see that novel, Catherine,'' she said when Payne's niece came back in the dining room. Just then his glance slid to Rainey's. Something was going on with his fiancée. She refused to leave the subject alone.

Catherine handed it to her before hurrying over to the buffet.

"Who wants to go for a sail after we're through eating?''

"We do!'' the girls said at the same time, thrilled over Payne's suggestion.

"What about you, Diane? It's a calm sea today.''

"I believe I will come with you.''

"That's great!'' Catherine enthused. ''We'll all get a tan together.''

"Give me a few minutes to get ready.'' She pushed her wheelchair away from the table and headed for the hallway.

"That's three out of four. Rainey? Does the idea appeal?''

Under other circumstances she couldn't imagine anything more exciting than going out on the ocean with him, but not now. Not ever.

While Diane was still in earshort she said, ''If we're

going to work together later, I'd better finish my greeting card project while you're gone. The deadline for the artwork is coming up soon.''

Payne's niece turned to her with an interested expression. ''What are you working on?''

''Right now, a bon voyage card showing a saucy Siamese cat with diamonds around her neck and red silk gloves up to her shoulders. She's stretched out on top of one of those mansard rooftops in an elegant arrondissement of Paris waving goodbye with her tail to a rascal of a mutt.''

''Oh how cute!'' Catherine cried.

''He has a hobo's stick over his shoulder. There's a little bag tied to the end with a Provençal print scarf. His beret is set at a jaunty angle.'' Rainey closed her eyes and shook her head. ''They're in love.''

The girls burst into laughter. So did Payne.

''Can we see it?'' Linda sounded as excited as Catherine.

''Of course. When you get back from sailing, come to my room. Have fun everybody.''

Grateful the girls were there to provide a buffer against Payne, Rainey left the dining room without looking at him. She hoped it didn't seem like she was running a marathon to get away from him.

For the next three hours she worked steadily on her sketches, but her body broke out in perspiration more than once anticipating the moment when she had to join Payne in his study.

Those had been hellish moments downstairs with his fiancée. She'd practically accused them outright of having an affair.

Tears filled Rainey's eyes. The poor thing had tried to handle her pain and outrage in a dignified manner. It was an awful experience. Rainey refused to put Diane through that again.

From here on out, Payne would have to deal with his fiancée on his own. Rainey would remain in the background a little while longer to work on his maps before she left for Colorado. That was it.

Eventually she heard footsteps in the hall. Payne had come back with the girls. Rainey invited them inside and let them look at her drawings.

Before they left to ride their bikes to Catherine's house, Rainey told Linda to come over on Tuesday morning after Payne left for Paris. Before she got to work she'd do a sketch of Linda and her dog, Hannibal, playing on the beach.

The three of them went downstairs together. Rainey saw them out. When she came back in the house Betty told her Payne had driven his fiancée home and would be back at one to get busy.

Rainey glanced at her watch. She had one hour. Now would be a good time to make a credit card call home and tell her parents what was going on.

Tomorrow she would buy herself a good cell phone. Then she could call her friends and give them a phone number without them knowing her new address. She would ask the post office to hold her mail.

For security reasons as well as personal ones, no one could know she was living temporarily at Crag's Head.

CHAPTER NINE

"DID you really have a good time out there, or were you putting up a front for the girls?"

The limousine would be pulling up in front of the Wylie estate before long.

Diane shot Payne a piercing glance. "Why do you bother to ask me a question like that when you know I hated it."

Payne rubbed his forehead. "Then why did you come sailing and put yourself through misery?"

"To please you. To spend some time with you."

"I realize we haven't had much time alone together lately, but I promised Phyllis I'd watch out for Catherine while they were away. They'll be home tomorrow night. Once I'm back from Paris next weekend, I'll be free for you. We'll do whatever needs doing to get ready for the wedding."

"How would you feel if I flew to Paris with you?"

To say that Payne was surprised by her question was putting it mildly. His fiancée hadn't wanted to go anywhere since the shooting. Though no one had said it, both his family and hers feared she was turning into a recluse.

There was only one reason for the drastic change in her. One person whose performance earlier today had sent thrills and chills through every centimeter of his body.

"Do you want to go with me to please me, or yourself, Diane?"

"Both," she answered honestly.

"Then there's nothing I'd like more." He meant it. If this was the beginning of a metamorphosis, he was overjoyed. Thank God for Rainey. He pressed a kiss to Diane's temple.

She laid her head against his shoulder. "I know you have business, but do you think you could take some time off to shop with me? I'm not that happy with the wedding dress I've picked out. Since we haven't had any pictures taken yet, maybe I'll see something there I like better."

"We'll do it. Would you like to bring someone to keep you company while I'm busy?"

"No. I want to see how I function on my own."

He squeezed her hand. "Good for you."

His elation was too great. He had to be careful. She hadn't mentioned Rainey. Whatever she was holding back would eventually come out, but he wasn't going to broach the subject right now. Not when they'd just entered new territory.

It was like tunneling underground, a precarious business at best. You never knew when the earth might cave in on you, entombing you in blackness.

When they reached the Wylie estate he helped her into the house. "I'll be at the office tomorrow. At some point I'll phone you and we'll make final plans for our trip. Would you like to see a play at the Comédie Française? I can call ahead and reserve tickets."

"I don't know. Why don't we decide what to do after we get there."

"Whatever you want."

The drive back to Crag's Head took long enough that by the time he walked through the house to find Rainey, some of his elation had worn off.

Today Diane had been provoked, and she'd rallied. The fact that she was willing to go anywhere at all constituted a miracle of sorts.

But Paris wasn't Switzerland.

Was it possible she was toying with him to pay him back for involving Rainey in their personal lives? Could it be Diane was pretending to go so far but no further when it came to the bottom line?

Payne didn't want to think the worst where she was concerned, however anything was possible.

"I guess I don't have to ask you how things went with Diane."

Rainey.

His head jerked to the right. He discovered her standing in front of one of his maps.

Every time he saw her, he felt like it was the first time. Something inside him ignited. The pulse throbbed at the base of his throat. It was an involuntary response, and there wasn't a damn thing he could do about it.

"Your fiancée is too intelligent not to have seen through your plan, Payne."

"Nevertheless she's going to Paris with me on Tuesday."

"Really?" she cried with a haunting smile. "Then why aren't you looking happier about it?"

He rubbed the back of his neck. "I don't know. Something isn't right. I've read articles about babies who never crawl. One day they just get up and start walking. But it's rare.

"That's what Diane did today. From recluse to transatlantic tourist, all in the space of a morning."

She moved toward him. "You hurt her by hiring me. I suppose it's not beyond the possibility that she's playing a game with you. But even if she is, your plan did provoke her to this much of a response. You should be rejoicing."

He had rejoiced. For a period of about ten minutes he'd allowed himself that luxury.

"And what if it's just a blip on the screen?"

"Then you'll try something else because it's the way Payne Sterling is made."

"Rainey," her name came out on a half groan. That adorable mouth of hers was such an enticement, he could barely concentrate. The urge to take her in his arms was so intense, he had to force himself to put distance between them.

"You want to know what my theory is?" she went on talking, oblivious to the powerful tremors that shook his body.

"What's that?" he asked with his back to her, struggling for control.

"The talk about romance novels got to her."

"Diane's never read one."

"Oh yes she has. Maybe not a Red Rose Romance, but her literature degree guarantees she's read the classics.

"The point is, since the shooting she's been in a depression and hasn't allowed herself to escape the reality of her situation. But the court hearing has forced her to listen to Catherine and Linda, even Nyla, go on about their favorite kinds of books.

"I believe their conversation has reminded her of your relationship before she got shot—w-when she felt whole and knew she was all things to you," she stammered.

Lord.

"Remember what Linda said? *It's fun to see how two completely different people get together, the problems they have to overcome.*

"Maybe Diane's not ready for an operation yet, but she's decided to go to Paris with you to prove she's trying to conquer her fear and be that vital woman you fell in love with."

His heart almost failed him. "You're wrong, Rainey."

There was a slight pause. "As I said, it was just a theory," her voice trailed.

He'd hurt her when it was the last thing under heaven he wanted to do.

Payne swung around, aware his breathing was ragged. "Where are you going?"

She paused midstride. Turning her blond head toward him she said, "You're obviously upset. I've only made matters worse."

"You're right. I am upset, but you're not the reason. Please stay. I need to talk to you."

There was a tender expression in her green eyes as she studied him. "Tell me about Diane. How did you two first meet? How long ago? I've wanted to know the answers to those questions since the hearing, but it wasn't any of my business."

Payne inhaled sharply. "Diane grew up on Long Island like I did. Our parents have always been good friends. They've traveled in the same circles, had parties with all their children at least half a dozen times every year for years."

"That explains so much," her voice shook. "You and Diane were—"

"*Not* childhood sweethearts," he cut her off. Payne couldn't let the lie continue any longer.

"I'm not in love with Diane. I was never in love with her. She only thinks she's in love with me."

Rainey's shock rendered her speechless. That was good. He had more to say.

"For the last ten years I've been so involved building my company, I can probably count on one hand the times I've even seen Diane in passing.

"During the last Christmas holiday her family invited mine for brunch. My parents asked them back for dinner. It's a tradition with them. I'd forgotten all about it because I stopped going to those functions by the time I went away to college.

"On the night Diane was shot, I was working at my office alone when I got a phone call from mother. She said Diane Wylie was on her way to my office. Apparently she'd been shopping and had lost track of the time. Would I let her in and bring her to the house for the annual party when I flew home?

"I didn't even know mother was having a party. It was the last thing I wanted to do, but if Diane was already downstairs in the foyer waiting for me to let her come up, I didn't see how I could get out of it. So I agreed."

Rainey looked shell-shocked. The way she was holding on to the back of one of the chairs, he had the strongest suspicion she needed the support.

"During the flight to Crag's Head we caught up on each other's news the way you do with an old acquaintance. She'd just come back from San Francisco where she'd been interviewed for an editor's job with a magazine there. But she'd decided not to take it.

"In a teasing way I made the comment that she'd probably met a man here and didn't want to leave him. She teased back that I could be right.

"At that point the helicopter landed. Mac had a flu bug and looked like death. I told him to go to bed. He argued with me, but I reminded him we were in the family compound which was secure. Nothing was going to happen."

The more Payne explained, the more he could see Rainey's complexion losing color.

"I decided to drive my own car for a change. We left straight for my parents' home a short distance away. I helped Diane out. We'd just reached the stairs of the house when someone called my name.

"When I spun around, I discovered a strange woman standing near the bushes brandishing a gun. I'd been stalked at least six times since college, but none of the women had ever been in possession of a weapon before.

"It was one of those surreal moments, Rainey. You know it's happening to you, but your brain is slow to react. I pushed Diane out of the way, then lunged for the woman. A shot rang out a split second before I tackled her to the ground. In the background I could hear Diane screaming that she'd been hit.

"Suddenly the whole world converged on us. Family, friends, security, police, paramedics.

"That shot shattered her world and mine."

"Oh, Payne—" Rainey moaned as if she'd been the one wounded.

"Diane didn't want anyone to touch her but me. It

was a fight to get her to relent enough to let the paramedics take over. Of course she was in shock.

"She clung to me like a frightened child, begging me to ride in the ambulance with her. I would have thought she'd want her parents, but I did what she asked because I was in shock myself and frantic for her."

"Of course. What a hideous moment for all of you."

"That's the word, Rainey. On the way to the hospital she kept saying that she was afraid she was going to die. Suddenly this whole confession came out that she'd always loved me and hoped to marry me one day."

Rainey bowed her head.

"Diane admitted that she'd gone to the city on purpose to see me. She used my mother by calling her up and pretending that she needed a ride home. Could my mother arrange for her to hook up with me?

"Her ruse worked," he ground out. "She accomplished her objective, but ended up paying a price no one should have to pay."

"No."

"That bullet was meant for me, Rainey. If I hadn't given Mac the night off, he would have dealt with the situation so fast that stalker wouldn't have known what hit her. That's what I pay him for.

"Out of all the nights to give him a break, it had to be that one."

"Stop crucifying yourself!"

"I don't know how. You'd think I would have learned from the other stalking experiences in my life that I'd always be a target and could never let down my guard.

"If you recall, God didn't say 'blessed are the rich

and the famous.' That's because He knew those tags carried a terrible price."

"Payne—"

"It's true. When all is said and done, I'm the reason Diane can't walk. The first two months were pure hell for her and for me. Every day I did a balancing act between my office and her hospital room. Each time I entered it, I prayed to hear she'd made a little progress.

"One evening while her doctor was doing rounds, he pulled me aside and told me there wasn't anything else they could do for her. But because she still had some feeling in her legs, he suggested she go to a clinic in Zurich which was renowned for a new kind of operation that was getting results.

"That was the news I'd been waiting for. When I asked the doctor if he'd told Diane about it, he said yes, but she was fighting the idea.

"I couldn't understand it, not if there was any possibility at all that she could walk again.

"Diane and I argued about it until she cried herself to sleep. When I went home I racked my brain trying to figure out how I could get her to change her mind and go."

"So you asked her to marry you," Rainey murmured.

Their eyes met for a long unsmiling moment.

"Yes. I thought my proposal would bring about the required miracle. I told her I'd take a month off. We'd combine her hospital stay with a honeymoon.

"Since our engagement she's said yes to the idea and then reneged a hundred times. We were still battling over it the day Catherine and Diane came flying into my brother-in-law's study to show me the cover on *Manhattan Merger.*"

"That was *my* fault," Rainey cried in anguish. "I should never have taken the risk of painting your face or anyone else's from memory!"

"Who's crucifying themselves now?"

"Touché," she whispered. "Payne—I—I have an idea."

"That's good, because I'm running out of them."

"In a few minutes I'm going to pack my bags and leave for good."

Rainey, Rainey.

"You think I didn't know you were going to say it before you did?"

"Please listen."

She was being all serious and noble. He folded his arms so he wouldn't be tempted to reach for her and never let her go.

"Behold your captive audience."

Like a nervous doe in the forest sensing danger, she backed away from him. "As soon as I've left in the helicopter, drive over to Diane's and surprise her.

"Tell her she was right, that you hired me to make her angry, and now you and I both realize the ploy failed miserably. Let her know I've gone back to Colorado, which is exactly where I'm going after I leave here.

"Then ask her to go away to Paris with you tomorrow instead of Tuesday. Tell her nothing's more important than her happiness, and that you'll never mention Switzerland again. I honestly believe if you do that, she'll find the strength to go to this clinic.

"I've seen evidence of that Wylie pride you were talking about. It means that deep down the *last* thing she wants is the Sterling name and your protection because she ended up in a wheelchair and you felt guilty about it.

"Like any real woman she wants your love, given freely.

"She knows the only way she can win that love is to fight for it *after* she's done everything in her power to stand on her own two feet first. That's why I'm convinced she'll end up doing what's best for her and you.

"And now I'm going to leave here because it's best for me." She started out of the study. "Will you tell your pilot I'll be ready for takeoff in ten minutes?"

Payne let her go. He had to. His commitment was to Diane. Rainey respected that commitment. She was an honorable woman. In fact she was so many wonderful things, he didn't dare start listing them or he'd never stop.

In less than ten minutes she was back downstairs again with her bags. They walked out of the house together without saying anything. When he'd put her belongings in the helicopter, he turned to help her inside. Her sunny smile would have fooled anyone except Payne.

"You don't ever need to worry about stumbling on to your life, Rainey Bennett. It lives inside you and infects everyone you meet."

Her eyes filmed over. "That's the nicest compliment anyone's ever paid me. For what it's worth, I meant what I said to Diane. You're a hero in every sense of the word. The next time I read a Red Rose Romance, I'll think of you, but I promise to control the urge to paint you."

The rotors whipped the air. It was time.

"Be happy," she whispered. Her kiss felt like the brush of a butterfly's wing against his jaw.

He closed the door and stepped away from the chopper. The noise it made rising in the air covered the groan coming from the deepest recesses of his soul.

When it was out of sight he broke into a run and headed for the beach. After a half hour's workout he went back to the house to shower and pack a bag.

Downstairs he found his housekeeper in the kitchen.

"Betty? There's been a change in plans. Rainey has decided to go home to Colorado. I'm leaving now and won't be back from Paris with Diane until next Saturday. Call me if there are any problems."

He phoned Andy to bring the limo around. Soon John and Mac had joined them for the ride to Payne's sister's house. He wanted to say goodbye to his niece in person.

Nyla happened to meet him in the hall and told him Catherine had gone over to the grandparents for Sunday dinner.

"Can I give her a message?"

"That's all right. I'll phone her over there. While I'm here, will you get me those paintings of Rainey's?"

"You bet. Just a minute."

While Payne waited, he called Catherine's cell phone.

"Hi, Uncle Payne!"

"Hi, sweetheart. I'm glad I caught you."

"Me too. I guess I left that romance at your house, but when I called Betty, she said she hadn't seen it. Do you have any idea where it might be?"

He frowned. "I remember Diane asking you to hand it to her. Maybe she still has it. If she does, I'll make sure it gets back to you."

"Thanks. How's everything going?" she whispered.

He swallowed hard. "Better than expected."

"Really?"

"Yes. I'm taking Diane to Paris with me in the morning."

"She's actually going to go on your jet with you?"

"That's right."

"Maybe this means—"

"Whatever it means, it's progress," he broke in. "Because of it, Rainey has decided not to work for me after all. She left to go back to Colorado a couple of hours ago."

A long silence ensued. "She was going to draw Linda's portrait on Tuesday."

Payne didn't know about that. "Tell Linda that Rainey would have done it if she could have."

"I will," she said in a quiet voice. "Uncle Payne? Are you all right?"

Don't ask me that, sweetheart. "I couldn't be better. If Diane can take this step, who knows where it will lead?"

"I'll keep my fingers crossed. I love you. Thanks for taking such good care of me."

Thank God for his niece. "I love you too. What do you want from Paris?"

"For you to be happy."

Someone else he loved had told him the same thing two hours ago.

"Ditto, sweetheart. Give everyone my love. Tell mom and dad I'll be by to see them next weekend."

"I will."

"Here you go," Nyla said as he put his phone back in his pocket.

Payne took the paintings from her. "Thanks for everything. My sister's lucky to have you.'' He gave her a hug before leaving the house with a precious treasure.

After he got to the office he would leave a note for his secretary to mail them to Rainey. They were her creation. She had the only right to them. If she decided to get rid of them, he didn't want to know about it.

''Andy? Take me to the Wylies'.''

Payne intended to follow Rainey's advice to the letter. He'd lost faith in his own instincts, but he believed in hers. She was the one gifted with second sight. Maybe she knew something he didn't.

Two days later he wrapped up a conference early with some of his engineers and returned to his apartment near the Place Vendôme. Thanks to the time Rainey had spent with him on the Paris map, he'd been able to give the men enough work to put them ahead of schedule.

''Diane? I'm back and ready to take you shopping for your wedding dress.''

''I'd rather stay in so we can talk.''

Payne frowned. Since Sunday when he'd surprised her, she'd been in better spirits than he'd seen her since the shooting. He didn't think he could handle it if she told him she wanted to go home. It would mean she'd slipped back into that immobilizing depression he dreaded.

He put down his briefcase. ''You don't sound like you're feeling well.''

When he walked in her bedroom, he found her seated in her wheelchair wearing a new two-toned pink suit.

''I like your outfit. You look very attractive.''

''I believe you actually meant that. Thank you.''

''I've never lied to you about your appearance,'' he

said as he sat down in one of the chairs next to her. "You were a pretty teenager who turned into a beautiful woman."

She eyed him directly. "I realize you've never lied to me. I'm afraid *I'm* the one who takes the honors in that department."

Her comment shocked him.

"When I told you I wanted to come to Paris with you, it was motivated by the lie I told myself about wanting to show an interest in your work. I've told myself a lot of lies, but that's all over."

"What's going on, Diane?"

"This." She held up *Manhattan Merger.*

Surprised he said, "Catherine was looking for it. She asked me if I would find out if you'd seen it."

"I put it in my purse when she wasn't looking because I wanted to read it."

Amazing. "Were you able to get through it?"

"Don't make a joke of this, Payne." Tears welled up in her eyes.

He reached for her hand. "I'm not. It's just that I know you prefer more meaty types of reading material."

"I do, but my curiosity was piqued. Little did I know the contents of this book would force me to see myself as I really am. It was a horrifying experience," she said in a tortured whisper. "Can you ever forgive me?"

"For what?" Payne was dumbfounded.

"For saying yes to your proposal. I placed you in an impossible situation. Ever since I read the last page of this book I've been waiting for you to come back to the apartment so I could do this."

She took off the diamond ring he'd given her and folded it in his palm. "I've robbed you of six months of your life. What's worse, you're such a good man, you were willing to sacrifice the rest of your life for a woman you've never loved and never could love. Not the way *I* want to be loved.

"The whole time I was reading this novel, I kept confusing the story line with our lives, Payne. Yours and mine and Rainey's."

He lowered his head.

"The look in your eyes when you introduced her to me... And then Sunday morning when the love for you came pouring out of hers...

"I could see both of you in the story, wanting each other, yet denying each other because Logan Townsend had a fiancée, and he was an honorable man.

"The only difference between that story and our lives is that I came to my senses first, and could release you from a commitment I should never have let you make. I know why you did it. The sin is on my head for lying to myself that it would all work out in the end."

"Diane—"

"Before you say anything, you need to know I've called my parents and told them the wedding is off. I shouldn't have been surprised to hear mother say she was relieved. They're going to fly to Paris tomorrow and take me to that clinic in Zurich.

"This book has made me realize that whether I ever walk again or not, I want a man to fall in love with me the way you fell in love with Rainey. The way Logan Townsend fell in love with the doctor who saved his life.

"If I hadn't tried to force something from you that wasn't there, I would never have been shot.

"My obsession over you was sick and wrong. In the end it cost us both unnecessary grief. It's humiliating to have to admit it, but you deserve to know that I recognize what I've done.

"Rainey knew a hero when she saw one in that group photo. She said the judge called it destiny. I *know* that's what it was.

"What if she hadn't painted you, Payne? It started a sequence of events that has freed you and me to live the lives we're supposed to live. Tell her I'm so glad she did it!"

For the first time since the shooting, Payne wrapped his arms around her because he wanted to. "I know you're going to walk again, Diane."

"I have to believe that too. I won't believe anything else." She hugged him hard, then pushed him away.

"What are you standing there for?" She smiled. "Pack your bags. I'm kicking you out of your own apartment because I happen to know there's a woman in Colorado who's dying with love for you. Go to her quickly. And please, please be happy."

CHAPTER TEN

"RAINEY?"

"Yes?"

She heard the zip open on her two man tent. "Are you asleep?"

"Not now," she muttered as Craig crawled inside.

"Liar. I heard you crying."

"Then I guess everybody else did too," she lamented.

"Don't worry about it."

He closed the zip, then sat down cross-legged on the floor in the semidarkness next to her sleeping bag. Now that the sun had gone down, it was cooling off fast. With the screened windows left open, it would be cold inside by morning.

"People are still being flown in. The ones already here are too excited for tomorrow's run to go to bed yet. Besides, I purposely placed your tent away from the others to give you some privacy. Are you ready to talk about Mr. Megabucks yet?"

"Please don't call him that."

"It was a term of endearment," he teased.

"He's anything but that kind of person."

"Tell me about him."

"Right now he's in Paris with his fiancée. They're getting married August first. H-he admitted he isn't in love with her." Suddenly it all came out in a torrent of words. Everything.

Craig let out a low whistle.

He put a hand on her arm. "That's tough."

She wiped the moisture off her cheeks. "After the hearing *you* were the person who told me that one day I'd look back on my big adventure and laugh about it. That counsel is the only thing holding me together."

"But it doesn't do anything for your pain right now. Still it's nice to hear I'm good for something."

"You're good for a lot of things." She sniffed. "Why else do you think I'm here? I'm just afraid you're going to be sorry I joined you on your last river trip."

"Are you kidding? I'm anxious to run some new ideas past you for the store. Tell you what? I can hear the helicopter coming now with the last bunch of tourists. If you're still awake after they're settled, we'll talk."

"Don't worry. I don't think I'm ever going to sleep again."

"Sure you will. After a day on the river tomorrow, you'll sleep like a baby."

"I hope you're right."

"Would I lie to you?"

"You never have before."

"There you go then. You want me to light your lantern?"

"That's all right. I have my flashlight if I need it."

"Okay."

When he left the tent, she lay down again. In this protected area of the canyon, the sound of the helicopter rotors reverberated more loudly than normal against the rocks.

She'd never hear one again without thinking of Payne. The sight of him growing smaller as his pilot whisked her away from Crag's Head filled her with such desolation, Rainey thought she couldn't bear it.

On a sob, she buried her face in the pillow.

The convulsions that shook her body were worse than ever. Her soul was inconsolable.

While she lay there racked in torment she heard the helicopter take off for Las Vegas. It wouldn't be long before her brother came back. She was glad because she knew she needed help to get through the night.

Finally she heard him undo the zip of her tent again.

"Craig?" she called out automatically as he crept inside.

"No. It's Payne."

"That's not funny, Craig."

"I agree," came a deep, familiar male voice.

Convinced she was hallucinating, Rainey grabbed her flashlight and turned it on.

When she saw Payne hunkered down next to her looking so handsome and alive, she let out a cry.

"Shh, darling." He brushed his mouth against hers before turning off the light.

She couldn't believe this was happening.

"I'll explain everything later. All you need to know is that I'm free. Diane has given us her blessing. Now come here to me and let me hold you, feel you."

Her heart thudded feverishly as he unzipped her sleeping bag and pulled her into his arms.

"Rainey—" he said her name on a ragged breath, kissing her in every conceivable place on her face and neck. "I've been living for this."

"I've been dying for it," she confessed against his lips.

Then she gave up her mouth to him and was lost in the fierce hunger of his kiss. They were both starving for each other.

She let out little moans of ecstasy. With each sound he drank more deeply until they were one throbbing entity of need.

Rainey clung to his rock-hard body, arms and legs entwined. Her lips roved over the unforgettable face she'd memorized in her dreams. Now she had the real thing to explore to her heart's desire.

"I love you," she whispered feverishly. "I love you with an ache that's never going to go away."

He cradled the back of her head, kissing her with refined savagery. Then he crushed her against him.

"I'm so in love with you, I don't know if there are words to describe how I feel."

"Those are the words I've been waiting to hear. I don't need any others."

She heard his sharp intake of breath. "Marry me, Rainey. I can't live without you."

"I wouldn't let you."

Once again they were devouring each other.

"You made a mistake crawling in here tonight. I'm already addicted to the taste and feel of you," she confessed when he allowed her to breathe again. "It's possible you'll never get out alive."

He buried his face in her neck. "You smell so good, Rainey. You feel so good. I love to look at you. Everything about you is a miracle."

In a lightning move he rolled her over so he was looking down at her. The full moon gave off enough light for them to see each other.

"Right now I can't see the color of your eyes. All I

can tell is that they're dark. At this moment you resemble my *Prince of Dreams*."

His white smile dazzled her. She'd never seen him look like that before.

That's when her breath caught.

The smile faded. "What's wrong, darling?"

"Nothing. It's just something I remembered when I'd finished painting the cover for *Manhattan Merger*."

He kissed the end of her nose. "What was that?"

"You were the embodiment of my dreams come to life on a piece of canvas.

"You had rich dark brown hair that looked vibrant to the touch.

"Your Nordic blue eyes seemed to envision things no one else could even imagine.

"Those rugged facial features denoted a life of hard work, sacrifice and triumphs.

"You had the build and stance of a conquerer beneath your business suit. Someone who dared to explore new frontiers.

"But you were a man who hadn't yet been transformed by a woman's love...

"When you smiled at me just now, I realized that was the ingredient that had been missing. It was missing when you were with Diane, but I refused to acknowledge it. If I were to paint you now, you would look different."

"That's because I am different," his voice shook. "You've transformed me until I don't know myself anymore."

His head descended. Once again they were kissing with a passion that was spiraling out of control.

"Rainey—" he cried. "I don't want to go down the river tomorrow."

"Neither do I."

"I want to meet your family as soon as possible."

"We'll go home in the morning and I'll introduce you. Mother's already a big fan of yours. Dad will be thrilled to learn that the great love of my life really is going to be the great love of my life."

Payne embraced her again. "He'll think this has gone way too far too fast," he murmured into her shimmery hair.

"So will your parents." She kissed his lips quiet. "But no man knows our history except you and me. After the tragedy that befell Diane in a split second's time, I don't want to waste any more of the moments destiny has allotted to us. Life is too precious."

"Amen to that."

He drew her to him in a possessive move that thrilled her to the tips of her toes. "You've never been with a man before have you."

"No. I've been waiting for the right one to come along."

"Oh, Rainey—" He rocked her back and forth for a minute. "Since I don't know how I can wait much longer to make you mine, we need to get married as soon as possible. Out of respect for Diane and her family's feelings, I want to keep it low profile."

"So do I. I've always planned to be married in our family's church. The timing is perfect. Craig will be through here the day after tomorrow."

"That will give my family time to fly out. Catherine will be overjoyed."

"She adores you, Payne, but then who doesn't."

Emotion made her throat swell. "Payne? Tell me about Diane."

She heard the deep sigh that came out of him before he turned so they were lying side by side and he could look at her. He traced the arch of her brow with his finger.

"Would you believe she took *Manhattan Merger* with her? When I got back to the apartment on Tuesday afternoon, she'd read it and was waiting for me."

"Oh, darling." Hot tears trickled out of the corners of her eyes. "I was afraid if she ever broke down to find out what was inside, she could be hurt by it."

"Hurt isn't quite the word. She was shaken with guilt."

For the next little while Rainey lay there in wonder while he told her how Diane had given him his freedom and asked for forgiveness.

She kissed his lips. "I'll pray she can walk again."

"We both will."

"I owe Diane my life. She let you go so we could have one," Rainey cried before breaking down in tears.

He held her tight against his heart. "She said the same thing about you. Your paintings put certain forces to work with the result that she wants to walk again and fall in love."

"One day I'll have to call Bonnie Wrigley and tell her everything. She'll be so thrilled to think one of her stories had such a life-changing effect on Diane."

"It changed all our lives, Rainey. I'll never underestimate the power of a romance novel again. Who knows? By the time you've become Mrs. Sterling, my sister Phyllis might be the next highbrow to crack."

Rainey flashed him a mysterious smile. "If she does, can I tell Grace Carlow?"

He gave her a passionate kiss. "Why is that so important?"

"Do you remember the question she asked right at the end of the hearing about how you found out your picture was on the cover in the first place?"

"I remember everything. That was the day Rainey Bennett entered my life."

She nestled closer to him, still unable to believe the man of her dreams held her in his arms.

"After court was over, Grace told Bonnie and me it would make Mr. Finauer's day to know Senator Sterling-Boyce's daughter and maid read Red Rose Romances."

Payne chuckled. "You're welcome to tell Ms. Carlow whatever you like."

"That reminds me I better get up and let Craig know we're not leaving with him in the morning."

"He already knows."

"How?"

"I had a little powwow with him before I climbed in your tent. He's already welcomed me to the family."

"I'm so happy I think I'm going to burst."

"Don't do that," he growled against her neck playfully. "I've got plans for us in the morning. The pilot's going to pick us up at eight. When we reach Las Vegas, we'll take the plane to Grand Junction. I've been anxious to meet my rival."

She frowned. "What do you mean? There's no other man in my life."

"Oh, yes, there is. According to your mother, you and this guy have been inseparable since you flew home from New York. I understand he sleeps in your bed."

''Winston?'' she half-squealed in delight.

''Who else?'' He chuckled. ''If he's going to live with us at Crag's Head, I want to start making friends with him now. If we can reach the point where he tolerates me, then we'll be doing well.''

''Tolerates you—''

Rainey wrapped her arms around him. ''He'll love you. He won't be able to help himself anymore than I can. Diane spoke the truth. I'm the proverbial putty in your hands.''

''Such heavenly putty.'' The kiss he gave her set her on fire. When he finally tore his lips from hers, she wasn't ready to let him go.

''Come on.'' His breathing had grown shallow. ''I don't trust myself in here with you any longer. Let's take a walk to the river and make plans while we wait for the sun to come up.''

It already has, darling. Don't you know the whole universe filled with light the moment you set foot in my tent?

The continuous clank of the buoy which marked the channel beyond Phantom Point brought Payne back to a cognizance of his surroundings.

He reached blindly for his bride of twenty-four hours, needing her like he needed air to breathe.

Instead of her warm luscious body gravitating to his, as it had done so many times throughout the night, he found a cool sheet. In place of the avid mouth he yearned to plunder all over again his lips met the pillows redolent of her fragrance.

Coming fully awake, he jackknifed to a sitting position. The semi-dark room below deck revealed he was alone. Maybe she was in the main salon off the galley.

"Rainey?"

No answer.

Though his thirty-five foot sloop was anchored in the bay, it still listed. The swells were bigger than usual.

Payne leaped to his feet and threw on a robe.

He called to her again. Still no response.

That sent him racing for the stairs. By the time he'd reached the deck, his heart was thudding at a sickening rate.

With whitecaps surrounding him, and no sign of his wife in the aft cockpit, a blackness started to engulf him as real as if he'd just been knocked overboard by the boom.

He dashed toward the foredeck on a run. *"Rainey?"* he shouted at the top of his lungs.

"I'm right here, darling!"

Her answering voice had to be the sweetest sound he'd ever heard in his life.

They met midship and fell into each other's arms. He crushed her to him, lifejacket, backpack and all.

"Dear God, I thought I'd lost you—" He was trembling so hard from fear he could hardly stand up. "Don't ever do that to me again."

"I won't— I promise—" Her voice shook. "I'm so sorry I frightened you, Payne. Forgive me."

He couldn't stop kissing her face and hair. "If anything had happened to you—"

She burrowed closer. "I swear I'll never knowingly do anything to alarm you like that again." She lifted wet green eyes to his. "After last night you *know* I love you more than life itself."

Last night...

He hadn't known what living was all about until last night. Her loving had made him feel reborn.

"You *are* my life, Rainey. When I reached for you a few minutes ago, and you weren't there—"

"It's because I love you so much. I wanted you to catch up on some sleep. While I waited for you to wake up I reached for my sketchbook. All these images were running through my head, but I needed more light so I came up on deck.

"The wind turned fierce a few minutes ago, so I put my things away and planned to bring you lunch in bed. I was just coming back when I heard your frantic voice. I thought maybe something horrible had happened to you and I couldn't get to you fast enough."

He felt the tremor that rocked her body and clung to her. "Something horrible *did* happen. You weren't there when I wanted you."

"That's exactly how I felt when the helicopter flew me away from Crag's Head and I knew I'd never see you again." Tears ran down her cheeks already wet from salt spray.

"That's all in the past," he whispered, kissing her with a hunger even greater than before. "You're my wife now, and I love your plan for lunch in bed. But the next time you feel an irresistible urge to sketch, tell me first. My heart won't be able to withstand this kind of punishment a second time."

"Neither will mine. I adore you, Payne. I couldn't live without you now."

"Then we understand each other," he whispered

against her lips. "Come on. Let's get out of this wind and take a nice warm shower."

Her cheeks filled with color. "If we do that first, you're going to be starving later."

He drew in a deep breath. "I'm starving now. For *you*."

Obeying a need that had grown out of control, he picked her up and carried her back down to their bedroom.

It wasn't until mid-afternoon that they surfaced to fix a meal together and take it back to bed. Once they'd eaten, his gorgeous wife curled up against him with her adorable blond head nestled between his neck and shoulder. He heard a sigh of contentment. Before he knew it, she'd fallen into a sound sleep.

And no wonder.

After their ten-thirty a.m. ceremony at Rainey's family church, followed by a meal at her parents' home, the pilot of his company jet had flown them and his family and bodyguards back to New York.

At that point he and Rainey had taken the helicopter to Crag's Head, where they'd immediately boarded the sloop so their honeymoon could begin.

Once out on the ocean, to give Rainey a view of their home from the water, he weighed anchor in the bay so he could give his bride his full attention.

Until the last few hours there'd been no sleep for either of them. Worried that he might have worn her out with his insatiable appetite for her, it thrilled him to realize her desire for him was every bit as boundless.

He'd married a talented, generous, deeply emotional woman whose passion for life thrilled him to his very soul. Marrying Rainey had set him on the adventure of a lifetime.

She wanted his baby right away. Secretly he'd wanted that too, but he'd told her he didn't want her to feel rushed. That's when she'd asked him to close his eyes while she handed him her sketchbook.

When she gave him permission to look, he looked. She'd entitled the drawing *Our First Little Engineer*. She'd drawn a six-month-old boy wearing boots and a hard hat. He was riding on top of Payne's shoulders. The likeness of father to son was unmistakable. It touched a place in his heart he hadn't known was there.

Rainey's green eyes blazed with light. "I did this the first night you stayed at my parents' house. Since I couldn't creep into bed with you, I did the next best thing to feel close to you."

He'd already been given proof his wife had second sight. Like pure revelation he knew that baby boy was destined to make an appearance at some point.

Putting the sketchbook aside, he'd reached for her. "No more 'next best thing'. I plan to give you so much closeness you'll cry for mercy."

"I'm afraid it's going to be the other way around," she admitted in a tremulous whisper.

"Then we're the luckiest man and woman alive."

"We are." Her voice caught before rapture consumed them for the rest of the night.

Payne drew her sleeping body close against him one more time. Then he laid her down and moved off the bed, compelled to see what she'd been drawing.

He found her backpack and pulled out the sketch pad. After studying the little engineer one more time, he turned to the next drawing and came face to face with himself.

It was the picture on the cover of *Manhattan Merger*. But there was a different woman in Payne's arms, a different look in his eyes. This time he held his adoring wife in his embrace. They both wore their wedding clothes. The gold band she'd given him was on his finger.

She wore his diamond ring and wedding band. The picture on his office wall had been changed to depict Crag's Head and the sailboat. There was another little picture propped on the desk next to Winston. It was Bruno.

The eager, tremulous look of joy on their faces brought tears to his eyes. She'd dated and titled it, *The Look of Love*.

Emotion made his throat close up.

"I wanted to capture our wedding night so we'd have it forever." Rainey had come up behind him and slid her arms around his chest. She pressed her cheek against his back. "I love you so much I never want to do anything to take that look away."

He put the sketchbook on the end of the bed. Turning in her arms, he cupped her precious face in his hands. "We'll hang this in our bedroom. It'll be our guiding star as we navigate through life together."

"Yes—" she cried as her eyes filled.

Payne lowered his head to taste those salty tears before he swept them away to the place destiny had reserved for them.

EPILOGUE

"RAINEY?"

"Yes, Betty?"

"There's someone here to see you."

Rainey was expecting her husband home any minute now. "Who is it?"

"They want it to be a surprise."

Because of security, no one dropped by Crag's Head unless they were family. Unless— Could it be Drew Wallace? He and his wife had been on vacation in Canada. Maybe he'd decided to pay her husband a personal visit now that he'd returned. The poor man was facing a mountain of work.

When Rainey reminded her husband he shouldn't be so gleeful about it, he reminded her that a mountain of work meant his company was still in business, for which they should be grateful. Coming from a soon-to-be trillionaire, that was quite a statement.

"I'll be right down, Betty."

At this point Rainey was eight months pregnant and didn't move nearly as fast as she once had. Sometimes she paused on the stairs to get rid of a leg cramp before taking another step. The calcium tablets were supposed to help, but she still had her moments.

Winston was so cute. He'd stop on the step with her and wait. She could tell Payne found it all very amusing. His blue eyes danced whenever he watched her struggle in an attempt to appear graceful.

He could hardly wait to be a father. They were going to have a boy. Catherine and Linda had already volunteered to baby-sit. Both sets of parents were ecstatic. Rainey's mother and father would fly out the minute she went into labor. Craig would come for the christening. Everything was ready for the big event.

Still wearing her artist's smock, which worked as a perfect maternity outfit, she put down her paintbrush and left the nursery to see who'd dropped by. With the addition of an owl peeking out of a large knothole in the tree, her mural of the forest creatures would be complete.

Winston stayed right with her. When she reached the bottom step and heard her name called, she turned in the direction of the living room. A beautiful long-legged brunette in a periwinkle suit started walking toward her.

"Diane—" she gasped incredulously. *"Look at you!"*

The other woman's smile was radiant. "I was going to say the same thing to *you.*"

She stopped in front of Rainey. They eyed each other for a long moment while unspoken messages flowed between them. Then they embraced each other. By the time they let go, they were both laughing and crying.

Rainey wiped her eyes. "You don't know—you just don't know what this is going to mean to Payne."

"Yes, I do." Diane insisted. "And seeing this will take away any residual pain." She lifted her left hand, where Rainey spied a gold band on her ring finger.

"I'm Mrs. Unte now. My husband, Karl, is one of the doctors I met at the clinic in Switzerland. We're expecting a baby too, but I'm only six weeks along."

Three miracles.

"We live in Zurich, but we're home for our first visit. If you can, I'd like you and Payne to come to my parents' house for dinner this evening. I know it's late notice, but we barely arrived and I couldn't wait to see you."

"I wouldn't have wanted you to wait!" Rainey's heart hammered with excitement. "I can hear the helicopter coming. Why don't you run out and issue your invitation in person?"

"You think it will be all right?"

"How can you even ask me that question?"

Diane smiled, then headed for the entrance hall. Rainey followed at a slower pace, marveling at the other woman's mobility after all she'd suffered.

This was a private moment for two people who'd been through a horrendous experience together. Rainey stood in the doorway to watch from a distance.

Payne couldn't help but see Diane now. The helicopter had landed. She ran toward it, waving her hands.

When Rainey saw her husband jump down and crush Diane in his arms, she could hardly breathe. Two or three minutes passed while the two of them conversed. Suddenly Payne swung her around. Their happy laughter filled the air.

Two people had been let out of prison.

Their joy was full. So was Rainey's.

She rested against the doorjamb, waiting for the most wonderful man alive to tell her all about it. She didn't have to wait long. The second Diane drove off, Payne came running.

As he drew closer she saw the one ingredient that had

been missing in their marriage. The look of peace. The one priceless gift needed to make their love complete.

She knew that was what he was trying to tell her as he pulled her into his arms and wept.

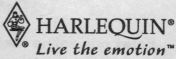

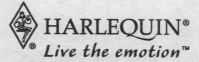

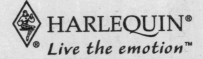

The world's bestselling romance series.

HARLEQUIN®
Presents

Seduction and Passion Guaranteed!

Your dream ticket to the vacation of a lifetime!

Why not relax and allow Harlequin Presents® to whisk you away
to stunning international locations with our new miniseries...

FOREIGN AFFAIRS

**Where irresistible men and sophisticated women
surrender to seduction under the golden sun.**

Don't miss this opportunity to
experience glamorous lifestyles
and exotic settings in:

Robyn Donald's
THE TEMPTRESS OF TARIKA BAY
on sale July, #2336

THE FRENCH COUNT'S MISTRESS
by Susan Stephens
on sale August, #2342

THE SPANIARD'S WOMAN
by Diana Hamilton
on sale September, #2346

THE ITALIAN MARRIAGE
by Kathryn Ross
on sale October, #2353

FOREIGN AFFAIRS... A world full of passion!

Pick up a Harlequin Presents® novel and you will enter a world
of spine-tingling passion and provocative, tantalizing romance!

Available wherever Harlequin books are sold.

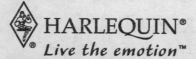

HARLEQUIN®
Live the emotion™

Visit us at www.eHarlequin.com

HPFAMA

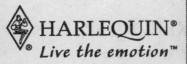

BETTY NEELS

Harlequin Romance® is proud to present this delightful story by Betty Neels. This wonderful novel is the climax of a unique career that saw Betty Neels become an international bestselling author, loved by millions of readers around the world.

A GOOD WIFE
(#3758)

Ivo van Doelen knew what he wanted—he simply needed to allow Serena Lightfoot time to come to the same conclusion. Now all he had to do was persuade Serena to accept his convenient proposal of marriage without her realizing he was already in love with her!

Don't miss this wonderful novel— brought to you by Harlequin Romance®!

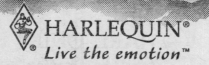

HARLEQUIN®
Live the emotion™

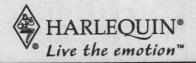